the Encore

Becoming Beka Book 5

the Encore

Sarah
Anne
Sumpolec

*To Judy -
Blessings to you!*
:)

Sarah Anne Sumpolec

MOODY PUBLISHERS
CHICAGO

© 2006 by
SARAH ANNE SUMPOLEC

Cover Designer: Barb Fisher, LeVan Fisher Design
Cover Image: Steve Gardner, www.pixelworksstudio.net
Editor: Cheryl Dunlop

Library of Congress Cataloging-in-Publication Data

Sumpolec, Sarah Anne.
    The encore / Sarah Anne Sumpolec.
      p. cm. — (Becoming Beka ; bk. 5)
    Summary: Beka has a lot to look forward to as high school graduation nears, but controversy over one of her songs creates havoc at school, a startling announcement shakes things up at home, and she and Lucy face serious boy problems.
    ISBN-13: 978-0-8024-6458-3
    [1. Dating (Social customs)—Fiction. 2. High schools—Fiction.
3. Schools—Fiction. 4. Christian life—Fiction. 5. Family life—Fiction.]
I. Title.

PZ7.S9563Enc 2006
[Fic]--dc22

                                                                    2005021670

We hope you enjoy this book from Moody Publishers. Our goal is to provide high-quality, thought-provoking books and products that connect truth to your real needs and challenges. For more information on other books and products written and produced from a biblical perspective, go to www. moodypublishers.com or write to:

Moody Publishers
820 N. LaSalle Boulevard
Chicago, IL 60610

ISBN: 0-8024-6458-0
ISBN-13: 978-0-8024-6458-3

1 3 5 7 9 10 8 6 4 2

Printed in the United States of America

For my Daddy, John T. Brewer.
For always asking.
For always being proud of who I am and what I do.
I miss you.

ACKNOWLEDGMENTS

Here we are, at the end of the series, and I'm overcome with a mixture of sorrow and joy. It has been such a joy to write Beka's story for all of you and to hear how it has touched your lives. You all are why I do what I do. Saying good-bye to Beka and the people in her life is hard and more than a little sad. I feel like I'm losing a good friend. I hope I get the chance one day to write down the next phase of Beka's journey.

A special thank-you to the entire team at Moody: Andy McGuire, Cheryl Dunlop, Barb Fisher for her amazing covers, and to everyone who helped Beka along. Thank you for believing in both me and this series.

Thank you to all my writing friends, you know who

you are, and to my agent Janet Kobobel Grant—for always moving me forward.

Thank you to my precious family: Jeff, Lydia, Cassie, and Molly—you are my heartbeat.

And then there is Jesus, the Author and Finisher of my faith. To You be all the praise and glory. It is in You that I live and breathe and have my being.

Sit down, Miss Madison." Mrs. Brynwit didn't even look up from her desk. I shuffled into the room and sank into the high-back wood chair in front of her desk. She moved one paper aside and picked up another, holding it in a pinch in front of her face.

I looked around at the dark, windowless office. I felt like I couldn't breathe. What could I possibly have done? It was the first day back from winter break, and I hadn't even made it to my seat in homeroom before Mrs. Lauden sent me to see Mrs. Brynwit, the principal.

She and I did not have a very good history.

She dropped the paper and stared at me for what

seemed like forever before she spoke. "This is becoming quite the habit with you."

"Excuse me?" I choked the words out. Somehow my mouth had dried up since entering the room.

"Well, after last year's events, the slanderous posts, the Snack Shack fire, well, frankly I thought you'd try to finish out your senior year without causing problems."

I lifted my eyebrows. "Excuse me? I, uh . . . I don't know what you mean. I've only been here for twenty minutes."

Mrs. Brynwit stood up and caught her hands behind her back—well, as best as she could since she had these short pudgy arms and a wide body. She paced in the narrow space between her desk and the bookcases.

"I've had a very serious complaint lodged against you. It seems one of the students felt their civil rights were violated by your proselytizing."

"Complaint? Prosta-what?"

Mrs. Brynwit stopped. "Proselytizing. Preaching." She picked up a paper and read, "'I was close to the edge, When You came to my rescue. . . . You came to me, Salvation in Your hand.' Is this not from the song you sang at the holiday concert?"

"Yes. It is, but . . ."

"And I assume you're speaking of God in this song?" Mrs. Brynwit sat back down and leaned forward.

"Yes." I pulled at my necklace and tried to take long slow breaths. Now if only the room would stop shrinking.

"This is a public school, Rebekah. This is not an appropriate venue for you to preach at the student body about your faith. Now there is one student I know of that was offended by your blatant disregard for other faiths, and there could be many more. Perhaps they were too upset to come forward."

I shook my head. "It was just a song."

"And even a song can make others feel like you are belittling their beliefs."

"You've got to be kidding."

"No. That's word for word what was in the complaint."

I felt sick to my stomach. How could this be happening? I thought everything was going pretty well. I made it through the holidays and my dad's engagement, and I mailed every last one of my college applications. It was like I had been punched in the stomach.

Then a thought occurred to me.

"Can I ask . . . who made the complaint?"

"That is none of your concern." Mrs. Brynwit looked horrified that I would even dare to ask.

"It's just. There's a girl who, well, she'd have personal reasons for making a false complaint. She doesn't like me. She hates me. Maybe she's doing it to get back at me."

Mrs. Brynwit straightened her back and pinched her lips together. "Miss Madison. It is none of your concern who made the complaint, because I found it to be valid enough to bring you in here. That is all you need be concerned about."

I sat stone-still hoping that she wouldn't try to suspend me again.

Mrs. Brynwit huffed and folded her arms on her desk. "So what do you have to say for yourself? Besides making more accusations?"

I chewed on my bottom lip for a second and tried to get my thoughts to calm down enough to answer. "It was an assignment. I just completed an assignment." I waited for another couple of seconds. "I got an A on it, too."

"Your grade is hardly the point." She spit the words out. What made her hate me so much?

I took a deep breath and said, "Well, the concert, well, it had songs from lots of different cultures and faiths. Mine was just one song. I guess I don't see why I'm in here when I'm not the only one who sang about God."

"I realize you are not the only one, but those other songs had been approved by the administration. Yours was not."

"Mr. Thompson knew about all of our projects. I turned in the lyrics weeks before the concert."

"And I will speak with Mr. Thompson about that. I just want to make it abundantly clear to you that you are not to engage in this kind of religious activity in my school. It's one thing to complete an assignment privately between a teacher and a student. It's quite another to publicly perform a song with such religious intonations."

I wasn't sure what she was saying.

"Are we clear?" she asked.

"I think so."

"Then get to class. I don't want to have you back in my office again, Miss Madison."

I grabbed my backpack and left before she could change her mind. The bell rang, and after checking the clock I walked to first period in a complete daze.

*   *   *

"I don't understand. So you can't sing your song again?" Lori took a bite of her sandwich and cocked her head at me.

Lori and I became friends back in the beginning of our junior year when she moved to Bragg County. And I was so glad for her right then.

"Well, yeah, but she made it sound like she didn't want me saying anything about God."

"Can she do that?" Lori reached back and secured her long dark hair into a ponytail and then rested her head on her hand.

I shrugged. "Well she did. It just stinks. I seriously thought I could get through a few more months of school without having some big crisis. I still have to wait to hear from colleges, then there's Dad's wedding." I shook my head. "It's still weird to say it out loud, you know?"

She nodded. "I can imagine. How are things with Gabby?"

I pushed the corn kernels around on my tray while I thought about it. I had hated Gabby at first. To be fair though, I probably would have hated any woman who showed my dad attention. It just hurt too much to think of him with anyone but my mother. It was coming up on two years since she had died in a car accident, and what started out as a friendship with a coworker had resulted in my dad's engagement and a wedding set for June 21. I had learned to tolerate Gabby and almost like her over the last six months or so, but it still felt odd . . . and wrong . . . to think about having a stepmother. It would be different for me though since I would leave for college in the fall. It was my two younger sisters, Lucy and Anna, who would actually be living full-time with a new step-mom. I was just glad I wasn't them.

"Beka? Hel-lo."

"Sorry. They're okay I guess. Not terrible, but not wonderful either. I like her as a person—just not sure about the stepmom thing."

"It's weird. Your family is planning a wedding and mine is planning a divorce." Lori shook her head and sighed.

"Are they seriously going through with it?"

"I don't know. Maybe. Dad is just so mad and he won't admit that it's serious. He thinks Mom and everybody else have blown it way out of proportion." Lori leaned back in her chair and folded her arms. "And you'll get mad if I say the other thing."

"It's not your fault, Lori."

"I know but it feels that way. I can't help but think that if I hadn't caught him looking at that junk on the computer none of this would have happened."

"Lori."

"I know, I know. It's just hard."

The bell rang and we gathered up our trash. I followed Lori to the door. Her shoulders were slumped, and I wished there was something I could do so that she wouldn't be so sad. She had only come to live with David and Megan Rollins a year and a half ago, and they adopted her within six months. Megan and David had seemed like a perfect couple, but then Lori had caught David using pornography. When she told, the marriage seemed to blow up. I understood why Lori felt responsible, but more than anything I wanted to knock some sense into David. By him not admitting what he did was wrong, it was making Lori miserable and destroying his marriage to Megan. How stupid could one man be?

I waved good-bye to Lori when we reached her class and felt a tug on the back of my shirt at the same time. I turned to see Mark try to duck away, but when I turned again, there he was, standing in front of me with a wry smile on his face.

"You got your hair cut," I said.

Mark ran his hand through his sandy blond hair and shrugged. "Mom made me."

Mark. It would help me a lot if he weren't so cute.

I started to walk and Mark moved to my side to walk with me.

"So," he said. "Loved all those phone calls you made to me over break. Yup. All those nice long talks . . ."

"I'm sorry. I just . . . well . . . I thought . . ." I had planned during the break exactly how I would respond to Mark when I saw him, and instead of my prepared speech flowing from my mouth, I felt tongue-tied and flustered. Why did he always do that to me?

"What gives?"

He didn't sound upset, but I felt bad for not being able to give him a straight answer. I liked Mark, probably too much, in fact, and even though we had been kind of on-again, off-again, when he was near me, there was no other place I wanted to be.

But it was just so complicated.

"We've been through this, haven't we? I wouldn't have known what to say if I had called you back." I crossed the hallway and opened my locker. Mark leaned up against the wall and watched me.

"We can sort it out. Let's try at least."

I sighed and shook my head. I closed my locker door and faced him. "We blew it, remember? My dad isn't going to let me go out with you because he says I'm irresponsible when I'm with you."

Mark stepped forward and wrapped his arm around my waist. "It never stopped us before."

"Mark."

"It's that guy. Josh. Is that it?"

"No. We're friends. Like I tried to tell you before."

I turned and walked away, but Mark appeared at my side a moment later.

"I saw you."

"Saw me what?" I swallowed hard.

"With him. At The Fire Escape."

"Yeah, so. We saw a movie."

"I'm just saying, I just didn't like the way you were looking at him."

I laughed out loud. "You've got nerve, Mark."

"What? I can't help it. I told you before break that I think we're meant to be together."

We reached the music room, where I was taking the second semester of music theory and Mark was a teacher's aide for Mr. Thompson. I found a seat among the random couches and chairs strewn across the large room, and Mark plopped into the seat next to me.

I rubbed my hands over my face and then dropped them into my lap. "You're going to make me have this conversation again, aren't you?"

Mark batted his eyelashes at me and a smile escaped

from my mouth. I tried to hide it, but Mark pointed at me and stood up.

"Ha! See, Beka. You can't deny it." Mark planted his hands on the arms of my chair and leaned in close enough for me to smell spearmint on his breath. "We can work this out." He moved all the way forward until he had kissed me and then walked toward Thompson's office.

My cheeks flushed as a couple of kids around me let out low whistles. I sank back into the chair. All I had wanted to do was have a normal end to my senior year. So much for normal.

*   *   *

We had a substitute for the class, which I thought was weird since it was the first day back from break. And I couldn't help but wonder if it had something to do with my song. Mr. Thompson had to just be sick—but I wasn't going to be able to rest until I found out. After class, I poked my head into Thompson's office and cleared my throat. Mark looked up and grinned.

"Where's Thompson today?"

"I don't know. Why?"

"No reason. Just wondering. See you later."

"Count on it." He waved and then turned back to his desk.

I fidgeted my way through my next class and spent most of the time in journalism trying to convince myself I had nothing to worry about. Mrs. Brynwit probably yelled at Thompson to make herself feel better, and that would be it. Since I was the senior editor for our student newspaper, *The Bragg About,* I was the one to make sure everything got finished in time to publish every Friday. It was a good thing that we didn't have a deadline this week though—it gave me more time to worry.

And Mai being in the class didn't help things either. She had tried to blackmail me into giving up my job at the paper, spread rumors about me, and told everyone that I had stayed in a psychiatric hospital during my junior year. I still didn't know why she was so popular. Gretchen Stanley used to be the popular one, and Mai was always following her around. But Gretchen had transferred to a different school and Mai had taken over as the queen bee. And boy did she have it in for me. I wasn't too happy with her either, because she had been trying to draw my sister Lucy into her crowd—which had nothing to do with wanting to be Lucy's friend and everything to do with Mai getting back at me.

Mai didn't speak to me at all during journalism, but she kept shooting me these looks that made the hair on my arms straighten. I thought maybe my overactive imagination was getting the better of me until I ran into her at the end of class. She sneered at me and then laughed as she walked away.

There wasn't a shred of doubt in my mind that Mai was the one who went to Mrs. Brynwit with that stupid complaint.

I walked by the office before I left just to see if there was anything out of the ordinary going on, but everything seemed quiet. I saw Mr. Stickel sitting at the duty desk in the lobby, reading a book. The teachers had to rotate desk duty all day just to make sure people didn't come in the building who weren't supposed to be there. Mr. Stickel helped Thompson out with the play every year, so I got to know him during *Annie* last year. I was debating about going and asking him if Thompson was okay when he looked up and caught my eye, waving me over.

"Hey, Mr. Stickel."

"Beka." He slipped his feet off the desk and sat up in

his chair. "So how come you didn't audition? You would have made a wonderful Peter Pan."

I felt myself blush. "Oh, well, I . . . I guess it's just not really my thing."

"Too bad. You really have talent."

"I got a song recorded." The words came flying out of my mouth. It would be so much better if I clammed up when I was nervous instead of spouting out too much information.

"Really? How did that happen?" Mr. Stickel stood up and shoved his hands into his pockets. His head came forward and tilted. He seemed to really want to know.

I cleared my throat. "Well, it's nothing really. I mean, a record producer heard my song at the holiday concert and had me record it so he could take it back to L.A. with him. It has to go before boards and committees and all sorts of stuff. It may be all for nothing."

Mr. Stickel wrinkled his eyebrows. "Why do you say that, Beka? You never know what could happen."

"True." I rocked onto my toes then back on my heels. "Oh, I wanted to ask you. Have you seen Mr. Thompson today? He was out. Is everything okay?"

"I'm not sure. He was in here earlier talking to Mrs. Brynwit. I'm not sure what's going on. He didn't teach his classes today?"

I shook my head.

Mr. Stickel shrugged. "I don't know. Sorry."

"That's okay." I saw Lucy come around the corner with a scowl on her face. "I better go. See you tomorrow."

"Good luck with your music, Beka."

I waved at him and waited by the door for Lucy to

catch up, but when she did she walked past me and right out the door. I sighed and followed her out, watching her auburn hair swing around her shoulders. This was getting old.

*   *   *

"What happened?" I asked after Lucy had slammed the car door closed and hunched down in her seat.

"What do you mean what happened?"

"Something must have. You were fine this morning, and now you're mad."

She huffed and turned away as I pulled out of the parking lot. I stayed quiet, trying to decide if I should push her or just leave her alone. I never knew what to do with Lucy anymore. My older brother Paul, who had moved to college for his freshman year, was always able to say the right thing to her. I always seemed to say the wrong thing. Even though she drove me nuts, I was worried about her.

When I pulled into the parking lot of the gym for her gymnastics practice she finally turned toward me.

"Beka. Can't *you* talk to Dad?"

"About what?"

"Me being grounded?" She rolled her eyes. "It's been weeks and he hasn't said anything."

"Why? What's going on?"

"I just have a . . . somewhere I want to go this weekend, that's all."

"Is that why you're in a bad mood? Cause you can't go to a party?"

"I didn't say it was a party."

"Lucy. Please. I'm not an idiot. Does this party have anything to do with Mai?"

Lucy crossed her arms and turned her face away. That answered my question.

"Lucy. I just . . ."

Lucy threw her hand up. "I don't want to hear this anymore. Mai thinks I'm cool, and just because you're not you can't totally mess up my social life. Besides, you're a senior. You'll be leaving anyway. I'm the one that has to stay here for three more years."

I took a deep breath and blew it out slowly. I knew Mai was just using Lucy to irritate me, but Lucy really thought she had been chosen for the cool crowd on her own. Mai and I went way back, and none of it was good. I knew she couldn't be trusted, but how was I supposed to convince Lucy of that? Especially when Mai was so good at lying.

"Dad's worried about you, Lucy. He doesn't want you to . . . things happen at those parties." I lowered my voice as if someone could actually hear us talking inside the car. "I caught you in a bedroom with Ethan, remember?"

"Are you deaf? I keep telling you I wasn't going to do anything with him." She threw up her hands and reached for the door handle.

I reached over and stopped her. "Can we talk about this more later? I want to . . ."

"What's the point? You never listen to me." She pushed me away and climbed out of the car, slamming the door shut behind her. I leaned back in my seat.

*   *   *

Lucy returned from practice and refused to talk to me, and then glared at me during dinner. Dad didn't even seem to notice. He rushed through dinner and then disappeared into the den to make some phone calls. I decided to just get it over with.

I knocked on her door. She had always shared a room with Anna until Paul went away to college. She convinced Dad to let her have Paul's room, and we moved his stuff to the basement rec room. Nobody was ever down there, and Paul would still have a place to stay during the holidays. Lucy was very protective of her new room, so I wasn't surprised to find it locked when I tried the handle.

I banged harder. "C'mon Lucy. Open up."

The door swung open and Lucy stopped short, her hair flying forward. "What?"

"Did you want to go over to youth group tonight?"

"I'm grounded, remember?"

"You're allowed to go to youth group. Come with me." I leaned on the door frame.

She growled and walked back to her bed where her books were spread out in a fan. I took a few steps into the room and took a seat on her trunk.

"Can we talk some more about this?"

"No. Not unless you're going to help me with Dad."

I dropped my head back and looked at the ceiling. "He's not going to let you go to a party anyway."

"He's not going to know about the party. I just wanted to spend the night at Amy's house." She smiled innocently.

"Yeah, right."

"Beka, I'm not doing anything that you haven't done."

Right between the eyes. She was right. "Not at your age. I never even left the house when I was your age."

She shrugged. "Well, I'm older than you were at my age."

"I just don't think you can handle it."

She scowled. "What is that supposed to mean?"

"These parties. The expectations. They revolve around drinking and sex. You're fourteen, Lucy."

"And you're not my mother." She looked down at her book pretending to read.

"I know that. But since Mom's gone someone's got to be straight with you. You've just been acting so different since you started at Bragg County. I don't know . . . I just want to help."

"Well, you're not. I need to finish."

"What about youth group?"

Lucy never even looked up.

"Whatever. If you need . . ." She wasn't listening anyway. I closed the door behind me and leaned against it. It was hard being the oldest sister. How did Paul manage, especially with Lucy? And why couldn't I seem to get it right?

Walking back to my room my thoughts flickered back to my encounter with Mrs. Brynwit. I still couldn't believe she had accused me of violating others' rights by performing my song. That night had been so special and so wonderful, and now it felt dirty and ruined. Even though I wasn't sure Mrs. Brynwit should have done it, I still didn't want to get in any more trouble with her or anybody else. I just wanted to finish my senior year. But the fact that Thompson was MIA on the first day back after winter break worried me. It just felt wrong.

I flicked on the light in my room and, as if on cue, my phone rang. I picked it up.

"Can we finish that conversation now?"

"Mark."

"Can I come in? It's too cold out here to talk."

"Where are you?"

"Looking at your window."

I walked to the window and looked down. Sure enough Mark was bobbing up and down in our yard, one hand to his ear and the other shoved into his pocket.

"I'm freezing, Beka. Give a guy a break."

My mind had a plan in an instant. Amazing how it worked so fast when it probably shouldn't.

"Go around to the basement door. I'll meet you there."

"Whatever you say, Beautiful."

I hung up and couldn't help but grin. It was nice to be chased.

I went downstairs and stopped by the den. Dad was bent over some papers at his big rolltop desk that sat in the corner of the den.

"You okay, Dad?" I stood in the doorway.

He looked up, his eyes tired and his hair messed up. "Sure, Butterfly. Everything okay?"

"I guess."

"What is it?"

"Oh, just some school stuff. But it can wait."

"Are you sure?" He motioned to his desk. "I've just got a lot on my plate tonight."

I flicked my hand. "No big deal. Well, I've got homework to finish."

"Okay. Night, sweetie."

"Night."

He was hunched over his laptop before I had even turned away. He'd never even know I was gone. I closed the basement door quietly behind me, leaving the lights off until I reached the back of the house. I unlocked the sliding glass door and then realized there was a broom handle in the way. Mark was pretending to freeze to death, so by the time I yanked the door open I was laughing. He fell into my arms.

"I thought you'd never come for me." He put his hands on my cheeks. "See, I told you I was freezing."

I pulled the door shut and Mark shrugged off his jacket. I led him into Paul's makeshift room. There was a small love seat, the bed, and a couple of chairs in the room, but before I could even decide where the best place to sit would be, Mark flopped onto the couch and pulled me down next to him, his arms around me.

"Much better."

"What are you doing here, you goof?" I adjusted myself so I could see him better.

"I wanted to finish our conversation."

I lifted my eyebrows. "Oh, really."

"Definitely." He leaned over and kissed me on the lips, then pulled back just a little bit. "I've been wanting to do that all day." He grinned and leaned back. I let out the breath I hadn't realized I was holding until that moment.

"You and I." He looked at me. "It's been a little crazy."

"You could say that," I said. "I just felt like you were . . ."

"Wait. I get to go first. Remember I'm the one that froze to death to get over here."

"Have at it." I leaned back, feeling even more pressure lift off me.

He opened and then closed his mouth, and then laughed.

"What?" I asked.

"I forgot everything I was going to say." He laughed and I joined in.

His laugh melted into a smile and he said softly, "See. We're good together. Don't you think?"

I rolled my eyes. "That's not what the problem is. You want to be more serious, and then you want to keep things light. You follow me around and then ignore me. I don't know what you want anymore. I don't even think you know what you want."

"Oh, I think I do. It's always been you, Beka."

I looked at him, the curve of his mouth, his deep brown eyes. What is it that I wanted? Did I want to be with him or not?

"You say you want me now, but for all I know you'll be dating Angela again saying, 'Let's keep it light.'"

"What about you? You can't make up your mind either," he said.

"Well, I haven't had to. You got mad about Josh and that dumb rumor and pushed me away. What was I supposed to do?"

Mark took my hand in his and rubbed the back of it.

He stared at it for a long second and then looked up at me. "Can we just start fresh? Last year. I don't know. It was all so crazy."

"True." A nagging image of Josh kept floating into my thoughts.

"So what about your dad? He won't let us see each other again?"

"He'll let me. He just doesn't like it. He doesn't want me breaking the rules."

"Then if we're more careful about that. . . . What do you say—can we try again?"

How could I say no? It all felt so good and right. I had lots of concerns, not the least of which was Josh, but Mark came after me. He was willing to take a risk with me, and that meant something.

"And you won't push . . . you know."

"I won't push." He rubbed his thumb down my cheek and brought my face toward his. "I promise." Then he kissed me again.

*　　　*　　　*

As I watched him trudge through my backyard, everything I felt so sure about a few minutes earlier began to seep out of me. Could I trust Mark? And what about Josh? Josh was three thousand miles away at college in Seattle and we had no commitments, even though he had hinted around that he cared about me.

I leaned my head on the cold glass and closed my eyes.

Lord, what am I supposed to do? I need You to be clear, to help me know which way to go. With Mark, it just seems so good when we're together and he really likes me. And when Josh was home that felt right, too. But now that Josh is away . . . I just don't know. And what if I make the wrong choice?

Lucy came down the stairs in a huff the next morning, but Dad barely looked up from the files he was staring at on the kitchen counter. Even Anna couldn't get his full attention. But Lucy sized up the situation and, on our way out the door, made a sneak attack.

"Hey Dad? Can I be done?"

"Done?" Dad took a huge sip of his coffee and looked at her.

"With my punishment. It's been weeks and you didn't say how long I had to be grounded and I want to spend the night with Amy Friday night and it's not fair to not know how long it's going to go on."

He seemed to consider it for a moment and then shrugged. "Sure, okay. But I don't want to have a next time. Got it?"

She grinned and nodded.

"No more breaking the rules?"

She shook her head.

"Fine, you can go to Amy's this weekend."

She threw her arms around Dad and he patted her head, but he had already picked up a legal pad and was studying it, frowning.

* * *

Lucy grinned all the way to school.

"So are you really going to Amy's?" I asked her on the way into the brick building.

"Of course I am."

"You're not planning on going anywhere else?"

"Of course not." She didn't look at me.

I knew she was lying. But I had my own problems to deal with.

As soon as we walked into the building I overheard a couple of kids talking. It made me forget all about Lucy.

"No, he's there right now," one girl said.

"Thompson? Why?" the other girl asked. The first girl was pulling the other one, so I followed them.

"He won't leave until Mrs. Brynwit comes out. C'mon. I want to see."

My stomach did a flip, but I kept following them to the office. Maybe a dozen or so kids were gathered at the windows and another five or so blocked the doorway to the office. The two girls pressed toward one of the windows, but I went straight for the door. I had to know what was happening.

I made my way to a spot where I could see and hear. Aaron let me squeeze in front of him. I knew him from my theory class.

"What'd I miss?" I whispered to him. I could see Thompson leaning on the counter, tapping the toe of his shoe into the carpet. He looked calm.

"He wants to talk to Brynwit, but she won't come out. She wants him to come in."

"How long has he been here?"

Aaron shrugged. "Maybe fifteen minutes."

We both watched, but the big scene consisted of Thompson standing there with his back to us and the secretaries looking back and forth between him and Brynwit's door.

"Would you tell her I'll wait all day if that's what it takes." Thompson turned toward the windows and gave a quick wave to us all. He sat down in one of the molded plastic chairs that lined the windows.

The homeroom bell rang. Everyone began whispering, and I looked around to see if anyone was leaving. A few kids drifted off—they had probably only stopped out of curiosity—but most everybody stayed put. I recognized some from working on the play during my junior year, and some of them played in the band with Thompson.

Thompson turned in his chair and then stood up and walked to the door. He leaned out a little bit.

"Go on to class you guys. Everything's going to be fine," he said.

"What's going on, T?" one person yelled.

"Yeah. You okay?" another voice asked.

Thompson held up his hand, but at that moment Mrs. Brynwit's door swung open, rattling the bookcase next to it. Her face was stormy, and I stepped a little to my right to hide behind Thompson, who turned around to face her.

"You are welcome to come to my office to continue our discussion." The words were laced with anger.

"Sorry. I can't have any more closed-door discussions about this. I have nothing to hide."

Mrs. Brynwit glared, and Thompson took a couple of steps forward, exposing me to her. She caught my eye, but I looked away.

"These students need to be in class. As do you."

T shrugged. "Fine. Then let's talk. I've been doing the same music program for ten years. Longer than you've lived in this town. My student projects are approved by me. I want you to stop nitpicking my music program to death."

"Mr. Thompson, I am responsible for everything. Everything that happens in this school I have to answer for. The complaints come to me."

"So send them to me." Thompson threw his arms out wide. "I just want to teach these kids. They can't learn if they can't express themselves."

"There is an approved list of music available . . ."

"Give me a break. The list of twenty songs that are too boring to offend anybody? Music is self-expression not . . ."

"Mr. Thompson. We will not discuss this further. If

34

you would like to set up an appoint . . ."

"You're not hearing me. I've written proposals and explanations and discussed this with you a dozen times. It needs to change."

Several kids yelled their agreement with Thompson, but when they did, Mrs. Brynwit flicked her eyes between us and Thompson.

"That's enough," she bellowed. "This discussion is over. Report to class immediately." She looked directly at Thompson. "Or you will be suspended."

There wasn't a peep from any of the students, and I could only see Thompson's back.

"That's how you're going to deal with this? With threats?" He shook his head and lifted an arm toward us. "They're kids. Why don't you try asking them what they think?"

"I will do no such thing." She stepped past Mr. Thompson and stepped in front of the door, right in front of me. "This is your last warning."

I was too scared to move. I shifted my eyes and saw that no one else was moving either. Mrs. Brynwit looked at us and then back at Thompson. I felt like the whole world had stopped.

"Mr. Thompson, don't test me."

Thompson shook his head and laughed. "Brilliant use of negotiating skills."

"This is not a joke," she said, then turned to us and yelled, "I suggest you all start moving to class."

Thompson turned and faced us all. "Please. Go to class. C'mon." Thompson opened his arms and moved us all out into the hallway. He looked back at Mrs. Brynwit, who was standing with her hands on her hips. "This isn't over."

We walked with Thompson down the hall, and kids started breaking off to go to class, some disappointed that it had ended.

I caught up to T and asked, "I need to know. Is this my fault?"

Thompson shook his head. "It's been brewing for a long time, Beka. It's not about your song, but about every student who wants to share their music. I'm sorry you got dragged into it though."

"It's okay." I reached my class and watched the last few students walk down the hall. I still had so many questions.

*   *   *

I hadn't even made it to my desk in journalism before Ms. Adams, the faculty advisor for the paper, came over to me.

"We've got a situation with a story."

"What?" I couldn't handle any more surprises.

"Mai has asked to be assigned the story about Mr. Thompson, even though you have Sabrina up next for news features. Sabrina wants the story and is upset, but Mai said she had already cleared it with you. We need to get this straightened out." Ms. Adams adjusted her glasses on her nose.

I walked over to my chair and dropped into it. I could make Mai really mad and tell Ms. Adams that she had lied about talking to me, or I could let Mai have the story and hope she didn't drag my name into it. Neither sounded like a good option.

"I'll talk to Sabrina. Maybe they could work together on it."

"Good idea." She grinned. "I knew there was a reason I chose you to be my student editor."

I closed my eyes and wished I could just disappear. Maybe I could take my GED and just graduate early. Anything.

Mai did not like having a partner assigned to her, but I hoped that Sabrina, who was an honest kind of girl, would keep Mai in line and the reporting truthful. I didn't mention Mai going to Ms. Adams behind my back. I didn't know if letting it slide was smart though.

*　　*　　*

It turned out the local paper beat us all to the story. Which in our defense was inevitable since we only published once a week. Thursday's paper had the headline "Teacher Challenges School Censorship." I read through the article at lightning speed. Thompson had obviously gone to the press, and it was bound to just make things worse. The article mentioned a song that had been challenged for its content, but it did not mention my name specifically. And most of the article was Thompson complaining about the heavy-handed administration stifling the creativity of the art students. I felt a weight lift off of me. It seemed like maybe I was going to be able to stay out of the worst of it.

Even though the paper hadn't identified my song,

someone at school had, and the minute I walked through the doors I knew Mai had been busy.

"Way to go, Madison," one boy yelled at me in an unfriendly way.

"Yeah, Thompson's the best teacher in this stupid school," his friend said, and then swore at me. My stomach flipped over and I felt frozen to the ground. I didn't know whether to stay or run. Before I could decide, Mark appeared at my side and took my arm.

"Don't worry. I've got you." Mark led me to my locker and then helped me with loading my backpack. I leaned against the wall. People were walking by making comments, some calling me names and some telling me that I was great for standing up for T. I felt like my head was swirling, feeling like both a hero and a villain at the same time. Then I saw Mai walking down the hallway with Theresa, Chrissy, and Liz.

I don't know where the courage came from.

I stepped in front of her. "You must be tired," I said.

Mai snorted, "Really? Why's that?"

"Well, you must have been up all night making phone calls. You were the only one who could have done this, you conniving little . . ."

"Okay, baby, let's go." Mark grabbed my arm and pulled me away.

Mai shook her head and laughed. "Pathetic," she said.

"What are you doing?" I said to Mark. "She did this. This is all her fault. I should be able to tell her exactly what I . . ."

"Beka, Beka, Beka. Calm down. Take a deep breath," Mark said.

I did what he said.

"Yelling at her isn't going to help anything. She wants you to get all riled up. Don't give her anything else."

Mark was right. But I still wanted to tell her off. For once I wanted to be able to tell my side of the story and not just keep up with the rumors. Mark smoothed my hair behind my ears and kissed my nose.

"I'm right here, okay. We'll get through this."

I nodded, swallowing the lump in my throat. Now that the anger had evaporated, all I wanted to do was curl up in a corner and cry.

*　　*　　*

I only made it to the end of the fourth period. It seemed like everywhere I went one person would blame me and another would congratulate me. In third period I found a note on my desk that said, "Maybe somebody ought to teach you a lesson." When Mark showed up to walk me to my next class I shook my head at him. "I can't do this. I'm going home."

"No problem. Wait in your car. I'll take care of everything."

I saw Lori on my way out and told her that I was going home.

"I understand. Maybe it will help to just get away from here for a while, let things settle down. Do you still want to come for the Bible study today? Remember?"

I nodded. "I may need some Bible therapy after today. No, I'll come. I'll have to come back and get Lucy anyway. I'm scared, Lori. I wish it would all just go away."

Lori shook her head. "I'm so sorry. If I can do anything, please tell me."

I nodded. I had almost forgotten about the Bible study. I had invited Nancy, a friend from church who also happened to be Josh's sister, to come, too. I couldn't miss it, and I figured that was probably a good thing.

I started to feel better as soon as I got outside. How was I going to make it to the end of the school year? I felt like I was on some possessed roller-coaster.

As I walked through the parking lot, I realized that there was something wrong with my car. I couldn't tell what was all over it until I got there. It had been covered with eggs and toilet paper and what looked like shaving cream.

I burst into tears.

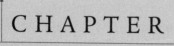
"*Oh, no.*" I heard Mark's voice behind me, but I couldn't bring myself to pull my hands away from my face. I felt his arm around my shoulder.

"I should go tell somebody about this," he said.

"No, please. Let's just go and get it cleaned. There's nothing permanent, right?" I took away one hand and peeked again at my poor little car.

"Doesn't look like it," he said. I watched Mark use the toilet paper to clean off the windshield as best as he could. "Let's just take it to a car wash. Is that okay?"

I dug the keys out of my pocket and tossed them to Mark.

I had stopped crying, but I still felt shaky. He kept

looking over at me on the drive but didn't ask me anything. He pulled into a do-it-yourself car wash, and he climbed out. His cheeks and nose turned pink from the cold as he scrubbed the car clean. Even though it was just my car, and not me, I still felt attacked. The shakiness and fear I felt after the episode on the beach had returned in full force. Would whoever did it come after me next?

I wanted high school to end. It was just all too much.

Mark climbed back in the car, pulled off his gloves, and warmed his hands by the heat vents. He looked at me and smiled with half of his mouth. How cute could one guy be?

"Thanks for cleaning it off," I said.

"No sweat. You okay?" He reached over and took my hand.

I shrugged.

"They're just trying to scare you."

"It worked."

Mark rubbed his hand along my cheek and then slid it under my chin. "It will be fine. I promise. T will get this sorted out. He's just mad."

"What if he doesn't? What if they fire him? Then everybody will blame me."

"This is not your fault. We'll figure out something."

We drove back to the school because I had to wait for Lucy, and Mark's car was still there. He pulled into a new parking spot and waited until we heard the bell to kiss me.

"Can I see you tonight?"

I shook my head. "I have a Bible study with Lori and then my counseling session."

Mark lifted his eyebrow.

"I told you about that," I said.

"I know. What about tomorrow? Are you coming to school?"

"I don't know."

"Well, I'll wait for you, okay? In the parking lot." He leaned over and kissed me again. "Call me if you need anything."

Mark closed the door and I slid over into the driver's seat. Lucy came out of the front doors with Amy, her best friend, and Mai and Theresa. I shook my head. I knew they were planning something. I felt this powerful need to protect Lucy, but at the same time I felt unable to do it. I would only be at Bragg County for a few more months, and then Lucy would be on her own. I wouldn't be around to watch out for her and make sure she didn't get into trouble. I watched Lucy wave at Mai as she left, and then she and Amy huddled together. After a few more minutes Lucy and Amy parted and Lucy spotted me in the car. The smile on her face fell away, and she replaced it with a smug look.

She climbed in and slammed the door.

"What were you and Mai chatting about?" I asked.

Lucy rolled her eyes and looked away.

"Fine, don't tell me. You're the one who's going to get hurt. Mai is just using you to irritate me."

"Oh, right. Everything's about you, isn't it? FYI, Mai could care less about you. You're the one who's obsessed with her. Gretchen's the one who burned down the Snack Shack and set up the attack on you. Not Mai. She was an innocent bystander."

I laughed out loud. "Mai innocent? If you believe that, you're even more gullible than I thought you were."

"Just stay out of my life, Beka."

I squeezed the steering wheel until my knuckles turned white. How dare she! All I wanted to do was help her. Mai was going to take Lucy in the wrong direction. I knew it.

*　　*　　*

Lucy refused to talk to me anymore, so I dropped her off at home and drove to Lori's house for the Bible study. We had been trying to organize it forever and we were just never able to sort it out. I sat in the car for a few minutes though, trying to gather my courage. Lori was inviting a friend of hers from her church and I had invited Nancy, Josh's sister and a sort-of friend from my church to join us. I liked Nancy, but she intimidated me a little bit, and it wasn't so long ago that we had a little run-in about her brother. She had apologized and everything, but I still felt uneasy. Especially considering my relationship with Mark.

I had no reason to feel guilty, but boy did I ever. Josh and I weren't a couple, but if Mark and I were now . . . I let my head drop onto the steering wheel. The worst part about it was that I wasn't going to be able to talk about it in front of Nancy. She seemed way surer of my relationship with Josh than I did. I knew she'd be hurt if she knew about Mark.

Why was life never easy and simple?

I looked up to see Nancy's car pull into the driveway

behind me. No more hiding for me. I climbed out of the car and gave her a small wave. She parked her car and waved back.

"I wasn't sure this was the right house. I'm so glad you were in the driveway!" She came over and gave me a hug.

Normally a hug wouldn't bother me, but today I felt like I wanted to run and hide. As if just by being near me she would be able to know every detail about Mark.

"Well, you found it."

Nancy looked at me and cocked her head. "You all right? You look a little pale."

"Oh, well. Just stuff at school. It's been a really crazy day."

She linked her arm with mine. "Well, that's why we're here, right? God can help us no matter how crazy our day is."

We walked to the door and Nancy kept chattering. "I'm so glad you invited me to come. My regular Bible study isn't meeting during the winter, and I love getting to meet new people. Where did you say your friend goes to church?"

Lori opened the door before I could answer.

"Hey, Beka. You must be Nancy," Lori said.

Lori's friend was already there, so all the introductions were made. Lori's mom, Megan, had made snacks, and she invited us all into the living room to get started.

I couldn't help but wonder how Megan was doing with everything. David still wasn't living at home, even though they were seeing a counselor to try to sort things out.

I always felt so weird in new groups. I never knew what to say, so I just let the rest of them chat, speaking only when asked a question. We spent the first ten minutes just getting to know each other. Nancy introduced herself and talked a little about being homeschooled. Lori's friend was Stephanie. She seemed sweet and, like Lori and I, also went to public school. She mentioned several boys in the first few minutes we were there, so I was glad to know I wouldn't be the only one with questions in that department. Nancy had been homeschooled her whole life and was already taking classes at the community college. She was one of those girls who had decided not to date at all and was big on the whole purity thing. I could actually feel myself blush remembering Mark's kisses in my car just a little while ago.

After Megan had prayed for us all, she wanted to know about the topics we were interested in studying. Fortunately, Stephanie blurted out "boys" and "dating," so I didn't have to. Then Megan asked if we had anything going on that we needed prayer for. I raised my hand.

I told them what had happened at school and to my car that day. "I'm really scared to go back. I mean, I'm seriously trying to figure out how I could finish my senior year at home."

"Wow, Beka. I didn't know your car got tortured," Lori said.

"What did they say when you reported the vandalism?" Nancy asked.

I shrugged. "I didn't report it. I just wanted to get out of there."

Megan was flipping through her Bible. "Here it is.

This is from Psalm 37. 'The salvation of the righteous comes from the Lord; he is their stronghold in time of trouble. The Lord helps them and delivers them; he delivers them from the wicked and saves them, because they take refuge in him.'"

We were all quiet for a moment.

"But what does that mean exactly?" I asked.

Megan looked around. "What do you all think?"

"I think it means that when we stay close to God, He'll help us through things," Stephanie said.

"Yeah, and look here in Psalm 32. It says, 'You are my hiding place; you will protect me from trouble and surround me with songs of deliverance,'" Lori said.

Nancy said, "There's a song we sing that talks about God being our hiding place." Nancy sang a verse of the song, and I closed my eyes and listened. A hiding place was exactly what I wanted.

"Well, let's all take turns praying for Beka," Megan said.

Everybody agreed, and they all scooted toward me at once. They prayed for me to have strength and courage, and they prayed for God to stop the enemy from stirring up trouble and for God to help the truth come out.

I felt much better after they prayed for me. That is, until Nancy took me aside just before we left.

"Talked to Josh last night," she said with a grin on her face.

"Oh." I tried to keep all emotion out of my face. Not an easy thing for me to do.

"He asked about you. He thought it was great that we were going to be doing a Bible study together." She paused and looked at me. "I really am okay with you and Josh now. I'm so sorry I was such a brat about it before. I just know how happy he is when he talks about you."

That stabbing feeling of guilt began to multiply inside of me.

"So how's he doing?"

"Good. He said his classes are hard but he's enjoying them. He loves Seattle."

"I know. He's mentioned that."

Nancy took a slow deep breath. "Would you tell me? I know it's none of my business but Josh is so vague it's frustrating. Do you two have an understanding?"

"What?"

"You know, have an understanding about your relationship?"

"We're friends, Nancy. That's all I'm sure about."

"Oh." She looked disappointed. "You two don't have any sort of commitment to each other?"

"No. We write to each other. And we saw each other those couple of times while he was home. But he hasn't really said anything."

"But you like him, right?"

I felt cornered. "We have fun together. He's a nice guy."

She shrugged. "I guess we'll just have to wait and see. I just thought that there was more going on when he mentioned that he was thinking of transferring closer to home."

"Seriously? He didn't say anything to me about that."

"Hmmm. Very interesting," she said.

I finally managed to get out of there and drive to my

counseling appointment, but the whole way there I kept thinking that Josh's vagueness was not interesting, it was making things downright confusing.

*　　*　　*

I had been seeing my counselor, Julie, for almost a year. Originally it was to help me after I had considered suicide, but she had been there to help me after my attack and with my dad dating and then proposing to Gabby. It was nice to have someone I could talk to about things and who could give me objective advice. She was the best thing that came out of my little bout with the psych hospital.

I filled her in on what was happening at school.

"My, my, Beka. You always manage to come in here with true dilemmas. My advice on this one—you need to go home and tell your dad about it so he can get involved with your principal. I would be willing to wager that she was completely out of line in confronting you like that."

"And what about the kids at school who think it's my fault that Thompson could be in trouble?"

"The truth is your friend, Beka. Don't be afraid to tell the truth."

"But they're not going to believe me." I buried my face in my hands.

"All you can do is tell the truth, Beka; you can't make them believe you. Worry about what you can do, not about what you can't do."

We talked for a long while about how to tackle this problem, but I never even brought up my Josh/Mark dilemma. And weirdly enough, that's what I really wanted to talk about. How sad was it that I get threatened and my car gets vandalized, and I was more worried about Mark and Josh? Did that make me normal or nuts?

*   *   *

I had to wait till after dinner to talk to Dad because he came in late. And once I saw him I added him to my list of worries. He seemed distant and upset, and he was working longer hours than normal. I wondered if maybe something was wrong between him and Gabby. We hadn't seen very much of her lately.

I waited until he had changed and settled in at his desk before I went to talk to him. I curled myself into the corner of the couch near his desk.

"Hey Butterfly. What do you need?"

He barely even looked up.

"Is everything all right, Dad? You seem kind of upset."

That got his attention. He laid down his pen and crossed his arms on his desk. "I'm sorry, honey. It's nothing you need to worry about."

"Is it Gabby? Is something wrong with the engagement?"

"No. No, she's just been busy out at her farm. She's having that new riding center built, and they've been having problems because of the bad weather. No, we're fine. It's not that."

"So what is it? If Paul were here you'd tell him."

He looked at me for a moment and smiled sadly. "You've got enough on your plate, Butterfly."

I stared him down.

He shook his head and sighed. "It's just some problems at work. Some rather big, rather messy problems. So you have nothing to worry about. But what's on your mind? How's school?"

I filled him in on what had happened at school with Mrs. Brynwit and Mr. Thompson and my car. Dad's face grew angrier as I told him. I was very glad that he was angry *for* me and not *at* me.

"I'll go to school with you tomorrow. We'll get this straightened out, honey. I promise."

I left feeling a little better. I wasn't sure it was going to help me with the kids who were mad, but maybe it would move things in the right direction.

At least it gave me some hope.

Beka. Beka. Beka. We don't have school! Look at all the snow!" Anna's voice shook me awake. I sat up in bed to see Anna at my window looking out.

"There isn't any school?"

"Nope!" She skipped across the room and out the door.

"That's the best news I've heard all week." I flopped back onto the bed grinning. I had the overwhelming sense that God really did love me. A whole long weekend away from school. Time always helped things like this, and getting three days before I had to go back—it felt like Christmas again.

My phone rang and I flipped over on my stomach to answer it.

"Good morning, Beautiful."

"Hey Mark."

"I have to see you today. What's going on?"

I giggled. I couldn't help it. "Mark. I'm not even out of bed yet. I have no idea."

"Okay. I'll call you back in an hour. I have to go help my dad shovel anyway."

"Bye."

We hung up and I rolled onto my back. Did I like Mark so much because he was here to give me all this attention?

My phone rang again. But this time it was Lori.

"I love all this snow. Kari Lynn is begging to go sledding. So what did you think of the Bible study?" she asked.

"I think it will be good. Of course, with Nancy there I can't talk about Mark. She asked me if there was any understanding between me and Josh yesterday before we left."

"What does that mean?"

"That's exactly what I thought. I guess she was fishing to see if Josh and I were official. Of course, I told her we're just friends."

"Right."

"It's not like he's ever asked me to be his girlfriend, or even said he wanted us to be exclusive. Lori, I'm so confused," I said.

"Because of Mark?"

"Partly. One thing Mark really has going for him is

that at least I know he likes me. With Josh I don't really know what to think."

"Have you thought about next year though? Yes, Mark is giving you his attention now and Josh is far away, but everything is going to change with college. And what about L.A.? For all you know you could be in L.A. recording an album in the fall. Boy, that's wild to say out loud, isn't it?"

"It's even weirder to hear."

"I'm just saying that everything is going to change, and even if you made some big decision right now, it doesn't mean that it's going to work. Long-distance relationships aren't easy."

"Speaking of?"

"Brian is great, but he's so busy. I just wish we got to see each other more."

"See, you applied to Tech because that's where Brian goes."

"Yeah, but that's not the only reason. They have exactly the language and international relations programs I want to take. If something happened and Brian and I broke up, I wouldn't regret my decision to go there."

"Why does everything always make sense in your life and nothing in mine does? You want to hear something sad? Mark and I never talk about our plans for next year. Of course, we weren't talking at all for a while. Maybe I need to bring it up. Maybe it will help me sort things out."

Lori said good-bye so that she could go outside with her little sister, and I flopped back into bed with no desire to get up. I was glad for the snow to escape school for an extra day. But how was I going to escape my own thoughts?

*   *   *

After Dad shoveled out the driveway and warmed up his car, he left for work. I was waiting for Mark to call back, and I planned to ask him to come to my house, thinking that only Anna was going to be around, but then I found Lucy watching TV.

"What are you doing here?" I asked.

She flipped the channels with the remote. "I live here."

"Duh. Why aren't you at the gym? You always go on snow days. Extra practice, all that?"

"Yeah, well, I'm not going today." She kept flipping through the channels, not looking at me.

"But your competitions. They're starting soon, right? When's your first one?" I sat down on the couch.

She was silent for several minutes.

"Lucy? When's the first one this year?"

"I don't know," she said. She stood up and went to the movie cabinet and took out a DVD.

"What do you mean you don't know?"

She whirled around, her eyes angry. "What's with the third degree? Leave me alone."

I watched her change the channel and drop back into the recliner to watch her movie. I sat back and waited. She was fourteen. I didn't have to obey her.

After a few minutes she turned around in her chair. "Still here?"

I shrugged.

"I dropped off the team. Happy?"

"No."

"Well, I'm done with gymnastics. It takes up my whole life. I want to have fun in high school. Now will you leave me alone?"

"Did you quit because of Mai?"

"No." She turned away from me again.

"Lucy. I want to help."

"I don't need your help." She picked up the remote and turned the TV louder.

If she didn't want my help, that was fine. But as long as I was around, I was going to try to keep her safe.

*   *   *

By the time Mark called back, I had a plan.

"I'm pretty sure she's going to go to a party tonight with Amy. Do you know where everybody's landing tonight?" I asked.

"I would think it's Liz's house. That's the only one I heard about."

Mark agreed to pick me up so that we could check in on Lucy later that night. When she left for Amy's before dinner she had that look on her face like she was planning something, so I had no doubt I'd find her at the party.

I spent some time in my room, alone. I sat in the middle of the floor with my guitar, picking out new melodies and making up words. The lyrics didn't flow perfectly, of course, but I always felt closest to God when I was singing to Him. If only I could understand Him better. I was trying so hard to keep my ears open to hear what God was telling me to do, but I really wasn't sure. After a while I set aside my guitar and read some of the Bible and prayed, but I still felt like I was missing something. How was I supposed to know what God wanted me to do? And even more importantly, did I want to do what God wanted me to do?

*   *   *

Gabby came over for dinner, and for the first time I was almost glad. Dad actually smiled a couple of times during the meal, and since she was going to stay for a while, I didn't feel bad about asking to leave.

"Dad, is it all right if Mark and I go out tonight?" Dad and Gabby both turned to look at me.

"Mark? I don't know, Beka."

"Dad, we've talked about this. You said if I followed the rules I could see him."

Dad sat down on the bar stool and folded his arms across his chest. He and Gabby exchanged a glance that I couldn't read. "I don't think a curfew is enough anymore. I think we need to talk about some more specific ground rules."

"What do you mean?" I had a bad feeling about this.

"For instance, I think you need to make sure you spend time in public places, not alone. If you're not alone you won't be tempted to . . ."

Gabby moved over next to him. She said, "I think she knows what the dangers are. Don't you, Beka?"

I felt my jaw clenching. Lucy was lying and probably getting ready for a party, and I was the one getting the lecture?

"I'm not doing anything wrong," I said.

"I didn't say you were, honey. I just want to be clear . . ."

"Dad, Mark and I have spent time alone already. Like tonight. We'll probably see a movie or something, but we'll still be alone."

"I know. I'm talking about spending time alone in his car, or at his house, or things like that. I don't want you to be put in a position where you might go farther than you should." Dad shifted in his seat. I could tell he was completely uncomfortable. Served him right.

"This is crazy-talk, Dad. I'm not the one you should be worried about. Lucy is the one that I found alone with a guy at a party, remember?"

"I know. And she was grounded."

"Yeah, well I'm not sure that did much good. You let her off."

"This is not about Lucy. This is about you and this boy. You're not . . . are you?"

"What?" I looked between him and Gabby. "Having sex?" They both nodded. "Puh-lease. Give me a little credit."

"And give me a break. This isn't the easiest thing for me to talk about either." Dad rubbed his hand over his face and then through his hair.

"Dad. I'm not having sex and I'm not planning on

having sex. But I like being with Mark, and he's waiting for me to call him back. Are we done?"

Dad nodded. "Yes." I turned to leave. "But we're going to have to keep talking about this," he called after me.

"Great. Sounds like fun," I muttered.

*   *   *

Mark and I decided to go eat first, and that gave me a chance to ask him the questions I had been trying to sort out all day. After we ordered, I took the plunge.

"So what are you going to do next year? Are you going to school?"

Mark laughed. "You sound like my mom."

"I don't mean to." I stirred the ice around in my Dr. Pepper. "School's going to end in a few months, and I wondered where that would leave us."

"We have more than four months, Beka. You worry so much." He rubbed my hand and smiled at me. "We just got back together. Let's just have fun."

"I'm not against having fun. Just tell me what your college plans are."

"I'm going to college. I don't have a choice. But my parents want me to go to a Christian college. They say they're worried about my 'spiritual health.'" He shook his head. "My parents don't get it."

"Get what?" I sat up, thinking this was important for me to pay attention to.

"Get me . . . and God. I just don't think the way they do. I believe in God, but I don't think He's got my whole life mapped out or anything. He gave us free will . . . choices. My life doesn't have to fit in some mold for me to be a believer. I think God and I are doing okay. He lets me do what I want, and I try and behave myself. It works for me."

I tried to keep my face calm and interested, but inside I was trying to figure out what he was saying. It was different than the things I had heard at church, and even though it made sense, something in what he said felt sour inside of me. Like it just didn't sit right.

"You don't think God has a plan?"

"Sure, a big picture kind of plan. But I don't think He cares where I go to college or what I major in or all that. As long as I'm living the way I'm supposed to . . . or at least trying to . . . then I think it's all good."

"I'm not sure I believe that."

"I know. But I think it's because you see following God as this narrow, gotta-do-it-this-way kind of thing. Kind of like my parents." He sat back in his chair, and I could feel his leg settle next to mine under the table.

"When we first met, I thought you liked that I stood my ground."

"I did. I do. I just think I'm a pretty good guy when it comes down to it. But I'm not perfect."

"I don't expect you to be perfect."

"Yeah you do. So do my parents." He had a sad look on his face that turned my heart into a puddle even though my mind was still trying to get a handle on what he was trying to say.

"I was just trying to find out where you were going to school. I didn't know you were mad at me."

Mark leaned forward and took both my hands. "I'm not mad. I want to be with you. You're smart, fun, and totally hot. What's not to like? I just don't take pressure very well sometimes."

"You think *I'm* pressuring *you*?" I had to hear this one.

"Well, why are we talking about the future? Why does it matter where I go to college?"

Wasn't the answer obvious? I narrowed my eyes at him. "How could it not matter? We're talking months into the future, not years. It's not like I'm asking where we'll be in five years or anything."

"I know. But we're still just kids. Dating. Having fun. I just don't see why we have to have some ultra-serious discussion."

"We're seniors. This is all everybody talks about." I folded my arms and looked around the restaurant. How did a simple conversation get so complicated?

I didn't know, but I wasn't about to stop there.

After we finished dinner Mark and I went to the movie theater, bought tickets, and then sat in a booth near the arcade until the movie started. It was still early and I knew the party wouldn't get going for a while anyway. I needed some more answers. Fortunately, the booth we had found was just around a corner, and it was at least quiet enough to talk.

"So what are we going to do if your sister's at this party? Drag her home again?"

"I don't know yet. But it'll at least put a detour in her plans tonight."

Mark laughed. "It's detouring my plans too."

"Oh really." I let Mark take my hands again. "I know

you're all 'let's have fun' and all that, but before this goes any further . . . well, can we finish talking about this?"

"What, the college thing?"

"No, the 'us' thing."

Mark dropped his head and then looked back at me shaking his head. "My Beka."

"That's just what I'm talking about. Maybe it's because I'm a girl, but I don't get this relationship. You say 'my Beka,' but what am I to you? You've said you love me, that you can't live without me, but you won't even discuss what you're doing after graduation. What gives?"

Mark slid out of the booth and moved over next to me, pulling me close. He leaned over and kissed me, sliding his hand up through my hair. I felt like someone had poured hot syrup inside of me.

He pulled away and looked me in the eye. "We're together. Isn't that all that's important?"

I wanted to scream "No!" But it was too late, he was kissing me again.

*　　*　　*

As we sat through the movie and Mark held my hand, all the questions came rushing back. Could I handle being with Mark when I had no idea when he might change his mind? He had done it before. When he was upset about hearing the false rumor that Josh and I were dating, he had gone out with Angela.

I didn't want him to promise to marry me or anything. But I didn't want to think I was spending all my time and energy with someone who might just disappear when he went away to college. Was that unfair of me? Or was it unfair of him?

* * *

The party was already pounding when we got there. I was worried about what some kids might say, but I was determined to keep an eye on Lucy.

Mark held my hand, and before we even closed the front door behind us, K.C., who was also a senior, draped his arm around Mark on the other side.

"Hey man, you made it. Cha!"

Mark winked at me and then looked at K.C. "You're ripped."

K.C. laughed and tripped forward. Mark put his arm out to keep him from falling, but K.C.'s eyes were locked on mine. He drew his eyebrows together and gave Mark's shoulder a small shove.

"Why's downer girl here? T's awesome and she shot the guy down." K.C. made the shape of a gun with his hand and pointed it at me. "No downers allowed."

Mark was every bit as tall as K.C., but K.C. easily had fifty pounds on Mark, probably because he played all kinds of sports. I felt like every nerve in my body went on high alert.

Mark slapped K.C. on the shoulder. "She's with me, man. Take it easy."

K.C. eyed Mark and then me again. I dropped my eyes to the floor. At least I was wearing sneakers. How fast could I run?

When I looked back up, K.C.'s expression was more

confused than angry, like he didn't even remember what he was talking about. I took the chance.

"I'm going to find Lucy. Don't disappear on me." I waved at Mark and made my way down the hallway. A couple of conversations stopped as I walked by, and I heard one person ask, "Isn't that the girl who got T in trouble?" I wished more kids actually read the newspaper. It would make my life so much easier. As soon as I stepped into the kitchen, I ran into another girl I recognized from my theory class.

"Beka! I'm so glad you're here! Kevin and I are organizing a petition to support T with, well, whatever he's trying to do. You'll help us, won't you? I think it's so cool that your song inspired him. Maybe we can even have a rally. I'll let you know on Monday. 'Kay?"

"Sure." I looked back at Mark, who was now partly surrounded by some other guys. I needed time to think, and here I was at a party looking for my sister. At least looking for her gave me an excuse not to think about how watching other couples kiss each other made me feel weird about letting Mark kiss me and, well, the way I kissed him back.

Every couple I walked past made me feel cheaper and dirtier. I was no better than any of them. *Focus.* I had to focus on Lucy. I was sure she was here.

I didn't run into Mai until I reached a room in the basement. She saw me and immediately leaned over and whispered in Jeremy's ear and laughed. I didn't want to even imagine what she was saying. Then I spotted Amy on the patio with a couple of other girls. I started for her when Theresa walked up next to me.

"I'm sorry about your car."

I turned and looked at her. "How would you know about . . ." I glanced over her shoulder to where Mai was sitting on the couch. "Mai did that? So it has nothing to do with the whole Thompson thing?"

"No. I mean *she* didn't do it. But I guess she . . . I . . . uh . . . I don't know . . ." Theresa stuttered and then left. At least some of it made sense now. I couldn't think about it right now though. Amy jumped when I grabbed her arm.

"Amy. Where's Lucy?"

"You scared me." She swung the drink she was holding behind her back.

"Where's Lucy?"

Amy shrugged, but I could tell she was nervous. She looked around. "I don't see her. She was here."

"I'm not playing games." I dragged Amy away from her little group to where I could threaten her in private. "Tell me where she is. I know where you live, Amy. I'll drive over there right now and tell your mom where you are."

Amy looked at me for a full ten seconds before she burst into tears.

"Don't tell my mom. Please. Please don't tell my mom."

I dropped my head back and sighed. Great. Just what I needed. A hysterical freshman on my hands.

"Amy, stop. I won't if you tell me where Lucy is."

"But Mai told me not to tell you. She said you'd show up."

"Amy."

"It's a loyalty thing. She's with him now."

"Loyalty? What are you talking about?"

"Mai said she had to, you know, prove herself. Prove that she wasn't a prude." Amy flicked her eyes away from mine.

"Where is she?" I yelled.

"Upstairs somewhere. I don't know." Amy started to cry again. "Now I'll never be cool."

"Amy. You'll only get their respect by losing yours. Don't do it." I shot Mai a look before I bolted up the stairs and didn't look back to see if she followed. I felt like I was reliving the last time I had gone through a stranger's house opening bedroom doors to find my sister. Halfway up the stairs I stopped and leaned on the banister. I couldn't keep doing this. I wasn't going to be here next year to drag her away from parties or out of bedrooms.

Lord, I don't know what to do. I don't know how she got like this, and I don't know how to stop it. But You do. I know You do. Help her, Lord.

I was about to head back up when I saw Lucy standing in the corner of the dining room with Ethan next to her and some other random kids around them. I walked back down the stairs and watched her from across the room. She wasn't smiling, and she was chewing on her fingers. Ethan was laughing and talking with the other kids, but Lucy just stood there.

She turned and saw me. She stopped chewing and let her hand fall to her side. She walked over to me and held her hands out, wrists together.

"Go ahead. Arrest me."

"For what?"

Lucy looked away and dropped her hands. "Just take me home. Please."

All the anger and frustration I felt toward her evaporated. I put my arm around her, and we went out the front door and sat on the front stoop. It was cold, but at least we were out of the house.

"Do you want to talk about it?"

She shook her head. She stared out in front of her with her arms wrapped around her legs.

"I didn't drive. I have to go get Mark. Will you be okay out here?"

She barely nodded. I left her and went back inside. It didn't take me long to find him, and when I did he was standing with Angela. She was leaning close with one hand on his chest. And he was smiling at her.

I couldn't deal with him, too.

I walked up to him. Angela jumped when I spoke. "I found her. You ready?" I smiled as I said it, but inside I was already planning the things I was going to say when I got him alone.

*   *   *

Lucy didn't speak at all on the drive home and didn't argue about going back to our house. I just let her sit. We took her by Amy's to get her stuff, and when we pulled in the driveway at home, she jumped right out and went inside.

"What's wrong, Beautiful? Is it Lucy?"

"Yes and no. It's you, too."

"Me? What did I do?" He looked genuinely surprised.

69

"Mark. I'm serious about needing to talk about this. Every time I try to have a conversation with you, you kiss me."

Mark grinned. "C'mon. You like that."

I couldn't deny that. "But that's not the point." I took a deep breath and blew it out.

"Is this about college? Look, I'll tell you all my plans if it'll make you feel better."

"Am I in those plans?"

He frowned. "I don't know. Do you want to be?"

"I don't know." I couldn't even figure out what I wanted to say now. Him standing with Angela, all of that seemed like no big deal.

Mark leaned forward. "Beka . . ."

I put my hand on his mouth. "You kissing me confuses me. I'm sorry but it does. It screws up my head and I can't even think about what I want to say." I looked at him with his big eyes and his dark-blond hair. He was so cute. And he liked me. Why should that pose some big problem for me? Why couldn't I just go with it? Have fun?

Mark leaned back and crossed his arms. I could tell he was getting frustrated by the way his lips thinned out. "What is it you want, Beka?"

"Tomorrow. Could we talk tomorrow? I've just got my mind on Lucy, and the stuff at school yesterday. I need some time to think."

"Okay. Tomorrow."

He didn't lean forward to kiss me, and even though that's what I wanted, part of me felt sad about it. I waved at him as he pulled out of the driveway but was unable to see if he waved back.

*   *   *

I went straight to Lucy's room and knocked on the door.

No answer. I knocked again. I tried the handle expecting it to be locked, but the door clicked open.

"Lucy?"

The room was dark, but because of the streetlights streaming through her window I could see her lying facedown on her bed.

"Lucy?"

She didn't move.

I walked over and sat near her feet. "Lucy. You don't have to talk if you don't want to. But if you want to I'll listen."

I watched her for any sign of movement, but after a while I gave up. She obviously wasn't going to talk, and I had my own problems to think about.

"Okay. Well, I'm going. But you know where to find me." I closed the door quietly and turned to find my dad standing behind me. I nearly wet my pants.

"Da-ad! What are you doing sneaking up on me like that?"

"Everything all right?" Dad pointed at Lucy's room.

I looked at the door and then back at him. "Sure. Yeah. Everything's fine. She just wanted to come home is all." At least that was true.

"I've got to go in tomorrow morning, so can you keep an eye on Anna tomorrow? Maybe drive her out to Gabby's so she can ride?"

I nodded. Dad kissed me on the cheek and went to his bedroom.

I felt so old.

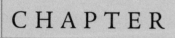
Dad left in a rush first thing in the morning, and before I had even swallowed my orange juice Anna was begging to go out to Gabby's farm.

"We'll go. I promise. But I can't leave right this second."

Anna stuck her bottom lip out and wandered around the house, letting me know that she was only waiting for me. Lucy hadn't come downstairs, so when I went up to get dressed I stopped by her room. Again she didn't answer, so I let myself in.

Lucy was still sprawled on the bed, but her eyes were closed and I could tell by her breathing she was sleeping. I took some paper from her desk and wrote her a note.

Luce,

I'm taking Anna out to Gabby's but I'll be back later. Do you want to go to the mall when I get back? Get some lunch?

Beka

I stuck the note to her forehead and went to get dressed.

*   *   *

Gabby was finishing up a group riding lesson when we arrived. She found us at Wind Dancer's stall a few minutes later.

"Gabby!" Anna threw her arms around Gabby. "Is the inside ring done yet?"

Gabby shook her head. "Nope, kiddo. They're still working on it." She looked at me. "Never believe construction workers when they give you a date."

"I'll remember that."

Anna grabbed her grooming bucket and began brushing her horse.

"I better get back. Can you bring her home later?" I asked Gabby.

"Absolutely. Your dad asked me to join y'all for dinner anyway." She tucked her hair behind her ear and rocked back and forth in her boots. She had made improvements in how she dressed away from her barns, but not so much while she was working. I understood, but flannel wasn't something I'd ever wear, even on a farm.

"Do you have a minute? I'd like to show you what I'm doing."

"Sure." I followed her out of the barn and around the side to where they were building an indoor riding ring. Gabby had talked about how much she had wanted one, and I could tell by the smile on her face how excited she was. I was happy for her, but farms and riding didn't thrill me like they did Anna. She toured me around and showed me the lighting and the stands and the new horse stalls she was adding. She had inherited the farm and then turned it into a successful business. And now she was going to marry my father.

"And over here, see, they're also adding onto the house. It was easier to go ahead and have them do all the construction at once." Gabby pointed to the extension on the house.

As the question formed in my head of why she needed an extension on the house, I realized the answer. My chest went tight.

"We're moving out here?" The words came out in a squeak.

Gabby looked at me surprised. "Yeah. Didn't . . . your father told you about that, right? It doesn't make any sense for me to commute here when Greg, I mean your dad can just commute to the bank."

I turned in a slow circle looking at Gabby's farm in a whole new way.

"You knew that, right?" Gabby looked worried.

I shook my head. "It just never came up. I thought, I thought you'd move in with us." I could feel the tears coming. I turned and walked away trying to swallow them, but it didn't work. Gabby didn't follow me, and as soon as I closed the door to my car, I let myself sob.

Even though it made sense for us to move here, I couldn't bear the thought that we wouldn't live in my house. That I wouldn't be able to come home to the very same kitchen where my mother made dinner, and to the rooms she cleaned. We had spent a whole Saturday painting my room together. All my memories were there. I couldn't do it. Making room for Gabby was one thing, this was something else. Losing my house would be like losing my mother all over again.

I closed my eyes and flipped through the images in my mind of my mom in every room of our house. Our family the way it was. I cried until I had nothing left. I felt stupid. Stupid for even thinking that Gabby would be the one to move. She couldn't. It made sense, but it was too horrible to even consider.

*　　　*　　　*

I drove home and checked on Lucy, who had shifted positions but was still in bed, and then I went to check my voice mail. There was a message from Mark.

"You and me. Today. Where are you anyway? Call me."

I dropped onto the edge of my bed. What was I going to say to him? Before I fell asleep last night I knew what I should do. I should break up with him. Tell him I care about him. Tell him that it would probably be better if we were just friends. But as thoughts of Gabby and my house and the farm came charging back in, a fresh set of tears started. I didn't want to get into a big argument with Mark. I just wanted to be held.

And Mark would do that.

I curled up with my pillow and stared at my wall for a while, trying to sort out my emotions and what I wanted. I didn't know what I wanted. It seemed wrong somehow to have whatever it was that was going on with Josh, and at the same time being with Mark. But even if I let go of Mark, it didn't mean that I could be with Josh. He was so far away.

If Josh and Mark were both a short drive away, who would I call? Who would I want to be with? That was the question I had to figure out the answer to. Then there was the whole problem of God. *What does God want me to do?*

And as soon as I thought it, I knew the answer.

But I didn't want to hear it.

*   *   *

The phone startled me awake ten minutes later. It was Mark.

"Where and when, Beautiful?"

"I don't know. Do you want to come pick me up, or we could just stay here?"

"I'll come over. In an hour or so. Is that okay?"

"Sure." I hung up the phone. I had the urge to write him a letter since I never seemed to do very well when I had to talk to him. Why had I ever let him back in my life in the first place? I had promised myself not to get sucked back in and here I was, right in the belly of the whale. And he was on his way over.

I wandered around the house, put away the dishes in the dishwasher, and plucked my eyebrows as I waited for Mark's Celica to pull into the driveway. I heard the shower going, so I knew Lucy was up, but I left her alone. I tried to pray, mostly for courage, and then went down to the basement to meet Mark at the back door.

He had a grin on his face.

As soon as I opened the door he pulled a small bag from behind his back.

"What's this?"

"Open it." He took off his coat and tossed it across an old Ping-Pong table that we never used.

I pulled the tissue out of the bag and found a butterfly Beanie Baby with a pink body and purple wings.

He put his hand over mine. "I just wanted to say I was sorry for last night. For not wanting to talk to you. I just got you back, and I'm already pushing you away. Will you forgive me?" He pulled my hand to his lips and kissed it.

How was I supposed to resist that? Everything I was sure of an hour ago seemed to blow out the door when Mark walked in.

"Let's sit. We'll talk and I won't push you away."

I followed Mark into Paul's bedroom and sat next to him on the love seat, but turned so that I could see him.

He clapped his hands. "College. That's what this is about, right?"

"Some of it, I guess."

"I applied to Tech, and then two Christian ones, Liberty and Berean University."

"Berean is where my brother goes."

"I know."

"So why'd you flip out last night when I asked?"

Mark leaned back on the couch and laced his hands on top of his head. "My parents are always bugging me about college. I guess I didn't want to talk about it."

"The Christian ones, are those your idea or your parents'?"

"You know me too well. My parents strongly insisted. What about you?"

I listed off the colleges I had applied to, leaving out Seattle. No reason to raise suspicions.

"See, we could end up at school together." He leaned closer, but I shifted to avoid a kiss.

"And if we don't?"

"Are you asking if we'll try long distance?"

"Maybe." I fiddled with the butterfly in my lap.

Mark sighed. "Beka. That's months and months away. Who knows what we'll be doing then." He scooted closer and put his hand on my cheek. "You can't try to figure everything out. You'll wipe yourself out. Let's just be together. We'll figure it out along the way."

*   *   *

I didn't push the conversation forward, because I didn't know what to say anymore. I wasn't trying to figure everything out, but giving a part of my heart to someone was a big deal to me, even if it wasn't to him. Maybe I was just scared of getting hurt, but I didn't trust Mark. He made me feel amazing and special, and scared.

We decided to go upstairs to watch a movie. Lucy had gone back into her room, so we had the house almost to ourselves. I felt guilty watching Mark pick a DVD out of the cabinet since Dad would have had a meltdown over him being here. But I really wasn't doing anything wrong, and even though Mark held my hand, he didn't even try to kiss me. It was a good thing too, since that would have sent me over the edge of confusion. I liked being with him. I could admit that. But I also wanted to see what it would be like to just be friends with Mark, enjoy him as a person, but there didn't seem to be a way to put everything in reverse.

At one point I leaned my head on his shoulder and he kissed the top of my head. It was nice. Maybe it was just me. Maybe I should just relax and see where things go.

*   *   *

After I walked Mark out to his car, I went to the mailbox and of course found a letter from Josh right in the middle of the stack. I laughed. God definitely had a sense of humor.

I waited until I got to my room and was curled up on my bed before sliding my finger under the envelope flap.

Dear Beka,

It was so great being at home and getting to see you, that it's hard to jump back into school here. Each semester is like being thrown into cold water. New professors, new schedule. This morning I walked all the way to a class I had last semester before I realized that not only did I not have that class, I didn't even have to get up that early this morning! I live in Ashton hall with probably 400 other kids. I'm not used to being around so many people and the campus is huge. I wonder sometimes if maybe I should have tried a smaller campus. I love SPU, but it feels so far from home. Have you heard anything from your record-producer, almost stepuncle yet? Please let me know when you hear, I'm praying for you. You have the voice of an angel and no matter what happens, I know God is going to shine through you.

On to what I really wanted to say today, and I'm so glad we're writing to each other because I don't think I'd have the nerve to say it if you were standing in front of me. I don't want to be presumptuous but I feel as if God has knit you into my heart. Everywhere I go I feel like I carry part of you with me. I know I'm far away and truthfully, that is what holds me back from asking for more than this—I want to know you. I feel like you hold back in your letters, and perhaps that is wise, but would you be willing to take a chance with me? Open up and see what God might have for the two of us? I'm not asking for any promises, and I trust that God within you will lead you, but I wanted to take the initiative—a word I've been learning a lot about lately—and be clear about my intentions. I want to have a deeper friendship with you, Beka, even if it can only be through letters for now. And in moving forward, I absolutely believe that God also will make His intentions for us known as well.

> *Unto Him,*
> *Josh*

I read the letter three times as if I was drinking hot chocolate on a cold day. Mark probably wasn't even home yet, and here I was reading this letter from another boy . . . or man. When did that happen anyway? Would turning eighteen this summer make me a woman, or would it take something else? Josh had always seemed like more of a man than a boy, from the first time I met him. And I had felt it even then. Didn't something inside of me know that something was different about the way he looked at me?

He wrote, "I trust that God within you will lead you." Would He? And would I know where that was? I had been all ready to tell Mark I wanted to slow things way down, to be friends, and all he had to do was walk in the door and I second-guessed myself. I didn't feel sure of anything.

I sat with my Bible and Josh's letter. It was one of those moments I wanted my mom to talk to. I needed someone who was wiser. I couldn't talk to my dad—he was so scattered with work, and Megan had enough going on that I didn't want to ask her. Gabby's face appeared in my thoughts, and I pushed the picture away. I couldn't talk to her. It would be too weird, too much like I needed her or something. It was one thing for me to admit that my dad needed her, but not me. When she moved in . . .

My stomach turned over. She wouldn't be moving in; we would be moving out. I looked around my room again, putting my mother in as many spots in my room as my memory allowed. Yes, there by the desk. She had sat there proofreading papers. And my dresser. How many times had I seen her bring in a stack of folded laundry and slip my clothes into the dresser? It wouldn't be the same anywhere else.

When I couldn't take the pressure in my chest anymore I relented and let the tears come again. I cried until I heard a knock at the door.

"Just a minute." I jumped up and looked in my mirror. My face was a hopeless wreck. No amount of cover-up was going to hide my red eyes and blotchy skin. Oh well. "Come in."

Gabby opened the door and looked around the corner. She had changed from her barn uniform into slacks and a sweater set. She looked halfway normal. "I just wanted to let you know we were here. Anna's getting cleaned up and your dad said we would all go out to eat tonight."

I nodded, trying to look busy straightening the makeup and perfume bottles.

"Beka. Can we talk? I'm sure you're upset about . . . about moving, and I honestly didn't realize that you didn't know. I'm sorry I shocked you like that."

"It's okay. I should have figured it out."

"No, we should have talked about it. I don't know, with the bank stuff and the construction . . . we blew it. I'm sorry."

I walked back over to my bed and leaned against my headboard. Gabby was still hovering in the doorway.

It looked like she didn't want to come in any farther unless she was invited. I didn't know if I wanted her to come in or not.

"You can come in," I offered. It seemed like the right thing to do.

Gabby looked relieved. "Thanks." She walked in a small circle, looking around the room before she sat in the chair at my desk. "I like your room. It's nice."

I gave a small smile and picked at the fuzz on the back of my butterfly pillow.

"So the moving thing, is that what you've been crying about?"

I shrugged with one shoulder. "Partly."

"I know you and me got a rough start, but I'm a pretty good listener. Isn't that how people get to know each other? Telling what's on their mind? Things that are bothering them?"

"I guess."

She leaned forward and whispered, "I've even been known to give some decent advice."

A small laugh escaped from my mouth, and she joined in.

"Is it a boy?"

"Two of them actually."

Gabby leaned back in the chair and crossed her legs. "Two? This I've got to hear."

"I got this today." I held up a letter. "And it kind of confuses things."

"So what's it say?"

I told Gabby the whole story, from the very beginning, and an hour later she was still listening and nodding. She had only asked a couple of questions, and as I got near the end I felt jittery about the way the story made me sound and I wondered if she'd think I was awful. Then a whole lot of other thoughts popped up in my head.

"So as soon as Mark left I got this in the mail." I handed her the letter.

"You're going to let me read this?"

I shrugged. "It's no big deal."

Gabby's eyes teared up. "No big deal? It's an honor." She wiped at her eyes and read through the letter. When she finished she folded it back up. "Wow."

"Yeah. But I don't know what to do."

Gabby looked confused. "What? Of course you do."

"No, I don't."

"Beka, you said that Josh is serious about his relationship with God and Mark isn't."

"Yeah."

"So you know what you should do. You're seventeen, heading off to college in the fall, your whole future in front of you. Maybe Mark's fun, but he's just a distraction for you, don't you think?"

I drew in a deep breath and leaned back on my pillows. Wasn't Mark more than a distraction? He was important to me, made me feel good. "It's not wrong to have fun, is it?"

"Depends on what kind of fun you're having. How physical are you with him?"

I let my mouth fall open and protested with a high-pitched cough. "I can't believe you just asked me that."

Gabby shrugged and looked apologetic. "Sorry. Someone has to, though. And I bet your dad has a hard time asking for the specifics. You said you weren't having sex, but there's lots of other things besides sex."

I rolled my eyes.

"You don't have to answer, but if anything that's going on makes you uncomfortable, that's another clue that maybe it's not the best thing for you."

After Gabby left, I looked down at Josh's letter, sliding my fingers across the folds. Josh had always felt so out of reach, and yet even three thousand miles away he was making an effort, making it known that he was interested. I didn't want to ruin that.

But I also knew that if I backed off Mark again it was going to make me look like an indecisive idiot. And he probably wouldn't give me another chance. What if I blew it with Mark, and Josh ended up with some college girl anyway? I'd be left all alone.

Seek Me first.

The words popped into my thoughts. Mark entered my life nearly the same time God did, and God was definitely getting the leftovers of my attention. And maybe I was missing out on something, too. The worst part about it was that Gabby was right. I did know what to do. I just wasn't sure I wanted to do it.

*   *   *

At church the next morning, Nancy tackled me before I had even taken my coat off.

"You won't believe this! My parents want to talk to your dad today, because Josh isn't coming home for Easter."

"What? Why would they need to talk to my dad about Josh not coming home?"

"Because we're flying out to see him! And they want you to come with us. It's a surprise, though, so you can't tell Josh. I mean it's a surprise about you coming, not about us coming. Isn't that great?"

I let the news soak in. Me, fly out to Seattle?

"And since Easter is so early this year we have to book the tickets now. That's why they've got to talk to your dad today."

"I wonder why they'd want me to come?"

"Duh." She pushed my arm playfully. "It means that Josh must talk about you more than you think." She grinned and hooked her arm with mine. "There are my parents—let's go find your dad."

Nancy dragged her mom and dad over to talk with my dad and Gabby. Nancy stayed with them, but I wandered away and watched from a distance, feeling out of sorts. After a while my dad walked over to me.

"So Butterfly. I guess you've been invited to Seattle."

I lifted my eyebrows and drew my mouth down. "Yeah, I guess."

Dad shifted and scratched his head. "Is there something I'm missing here? I thought you were dating Mark now."

"Josh and I are friends."

"Oh. Well. We don't really have any plans, so if you want to go, that's fine. Mike and Terri said they'd watch out for you, and since you applied to Seattle Pacific it's a great chance to see the school. Not that I want you to actually go there. Apparently they need to buy the tickets soon, so we'll have to let them know by Wednesday." Dad touched my face. "You're growing up so fast. You remind me more of your mom every day."

I leaned in and wrapped my arms around him. He squeezed tight. I could have stayed like that a lot longer than we did, but he let go and we walked together into the sanctuary. For some reason, I felt a sudden urge to tell him that something was really wrong with Lucy. She had said she was sick, and Dad had let her stay home. I would give it one more try before I told him though. He had enough to worry about.

*   *   *

Lucy refused to talk to me again, but at least she had showered and changed her clothes. I couldn't force her to talk to me. She had been much easier to deal with in middle school. It was like she had morphed into someone else when she became a freshman, and the girl who talked about God all the time rarely even mentioned Him anymore. And when she did, it didn't sound like she was doing very well in that area.

I went to my room and decided to work on writing Josh back.

> Dear Josh,
>
> Your letter came the other day and I hardly even know where to start. I guess I have to start with being honest. I've wondered for a long time exactly what it is "we" are and maybe that's why I hold back some.

I chewed on my pencil. How honest should I be? Josh knew about Mark, sort of. I just needed to write it. Be honest and see what happened.

> That and I wonder how you'd really feel about me if you knew me better. I honestly think you could do a lot better than me. I'm new at this whole God thing. I still get confused and even though I'm glad that you "trust God in me," I'm not sure you should. I blew it just this week.

I didn't want to admit that I had seen Mark this week, but I had to; otherwise I'd be lying to him. Right?

Mark, you've met him before, and I have dated off and on, mostly off. We weren't even really speaking to each other for a long time, but last week when school started up again he showed up saying that we belonged together and all this other stuff. And I just got sucked right back in, and now we've gone out a couple of times. I didn't even mean for it to happen, but it did. I'm just not a very strong person. And I didn't understand where we were at, and I could make a million excuses but it really comes down to this: I don't think I should really be with Mark—he's not good for me. I know that. But for some reason when he's around I completely forget that. See? That's why I say you could do a lot better than me.

I am going to tell Mark that we can only be friends. It's what I know I have to do no matter what happens with you and me. But Josh, seriously, here's a free out. I'll understand if you want to take back what you said after hearing all this.

And if all this doesn't matter to you and you still want to get to know me, then how could it work? What could we be to each other, other than pen pals, when we're this far away?

I do care for you Josh. I really do. But I don't want you to miss out on something because of me. I don't know what else to say, so I'll end this now. Please write back though, and let me know what you think.

> *Take care of you,*
> *Beka*

I read the letter three times. I wanted to change it, fix it somehow, but it was honest and I wasn't holding back, so I folded it and sealed the envelope before I could change my mind. Mail wouldn't go out until the morning, but I still addressed, stamped, and put it in our mailbox with the flag up. There was no turning back now.

When I came back in, Lucy was heading back up the stairs to her room. I followed her up.

"Hey Lucy. Are you feeling better?"

She didn't turn around, but when she went in her room she left the door open. I followed her in.

"So." I sank into her big beanbag chair that was in the center of her room.

"So what?" Lucy dug a book out of her book bag and carried it back to her bed.

"Are you okay? Do you want to talk about Friday night?"

"No. And why do you always want to have some deep discussion about everything? I have homework to finish." She didn't even glance at me.

"Lucy. I love you. I want to help. What's happened to you?"

"Nothing." She flipped the book open and held it in front of her.

I stood up. "All right. I'll stop bugging you. But you know where I am if you change your mind." I closed the door behind me as I left.

*   *   *

On Monday morning I had nearly forgotten about the letter sitting in the mailbox because I was so nervous about what would happen at school. After another article about Thompson in Sunday's paper, I knew the whole mess wasn't my fault, and that even my car getting egged was probably just Mai and not some angry band member. Dad had forgotten about taking me to school, and I didn't remind him about it. He seemed so distant and worried all the time that if there was any way to handle this on my own I figured I should. Lucy sat silently next to me on the way to school, and as we turned down the residential street that led to the school parking lot, I saw a large crowd gathered on the corner. We drove past, but I couldn't tell what was going on.

I parked and told Lucy I was going to walk back to the corner. She shrugged and left while I hitched my book bag up on my shoulder and walked toward the commotion. As I got close I could see at least one news crew. I spotted Mark watching from near somebody's fence. He waved when he saw me, so I walked over and joined him. His arms were crossed and he looked serious.

"What's going on?"

"Thompson's in there." Mark pointed into the crowd. "He's protesting off of school property."

I sighed heavily. "I wish this all would just go away. Why can't he just let this go?"

Mark took my arm and pulled me close to him. "You should know. He's doing it so that kids like us can sing whatever we want."

I watched and every once in a while I caught a glimpse of him. Reporters stood in front of him asking questions I couldn't hear and scribbling in small notebooks. I could only see the back of Thompson's bald head, but he seemed calm, sitting on a big blue blanket.

"Hey. What's she doing here?"

I heard the voices before I saw them. A girl walked toward me and two guys followed close behind her. Mark pulled me tight, letting me know he was there.

"Haven't you caused enough problems?" the girl said.

I stood frozen.

"This is all your fault," she continued. "If he gets fired, I swear I'm going to . . ."

"Kenzie, it's not like that. T said it had nothing to do with her," someone said.

"But it's her fault he decided to go AWOL," she said.

"Excuse me." A tall woman with blonde hair and a bright blue suit stuck her head in between us, the three of them on one side and Mark and I on the other. She smiled a big fake smile. "Couldn't help but overhear. Why did you say it is her fault?"

"Her song started all this," Kenzie said, pointing at me.

"Really? So you're the girl with the song." She turned away. "Sam!" A man with a camera on his shoulder hurried over and handed her a microphone.

"Can I ask you a couple of questions?" She held the microphone in front of me. In an instant, the crowd of reporters who were hovering around Thompson surrounded us all, calling out questions.

"What was the song about?"

"Why was there a problem?"

"What do you think about the protest?"

"What's your name?"

If Mark hadn't been holding my arm, I would have run.

I couldn't think of one intelligent thing to say.

"Who are you?" one of the reporters yelled to Mark.

"I'm her boyfriend," Mark said. "And you all need to leave her alone."

"You're my what?" I turned to Mark.

He whispered, "Shhh. It's okay, baby."

"It's not okay. Don't tell them things that aren't true."

"What's your name, miss?" a tiny guy with glasses and a tan suit asked, his pen poised over his notebook. Everybody quieted down to hear the answer.

As I tried to think of how to keep my name out of it,

the girl who first came up with the two guys yelled out, "It's Madison. Becky Madison."

"Bek-a," I said. "Not Becky." But nobody heard me because they started yelling questions again. I felt claustrophobic. There were too many people. Then I saw Thompson push his way in.

"Can we leave this student out of it? Please? This has nothing to do with her in particular, though I'm grateful that she finally helped me to see how disrespectful the current administration is toward the arts and the creativity of our students. If you have questions, ask me." Thompson winked at me then moved back toward his blanket, and the reporters looked between us like they weren't sure they wanted to give up their new lead.

I pulled away from Mark and followed Mr. Thompson. He sat down on his blanket, and because it was weird looking down at him, I knelt down beside him. "Thanks T but . . . I do feel like this is my fault."

"It's not your fault, Beka. This needed to happen. Controversy is good sometimes. It shakes us up. Reminds us to take stock of what's important. My students being able to sing their songs, find their voice—that's important. Not just yours, but everybody that's going to come after you."

"Miss Madison, are you joining the protest?" Another male reporter pointed at me and lifted his eyebrows. I looked around at all the reporters watching and waiting, and I could see the little red light on the news camera, probably filming my every move.

"Beka, go ahead and go to school. This will all be over before you know it."

I looked at Thompson, who looked more like a regular man instead of a teacher at that moment.

Then I smiled. "Yes, it will."

I let my bag fall off my shoulder and sat down on the blanket, making a show of making myself comfortable.

"Why are you joining the protest, Miss Madison?" the lady in the blue suit asked, holding out her microphone.

"Mr. Thompson's right. This isn't about me. It's about the music."

The kids in the crowd were murmuring and nodding their heads, and the reporters were writing furiously.

"What are you trying to accomplish?"

"What was your song about?"

"What was the restriction placed by the administration?"

I let the questions come. Thompson looked at me and smiled but shook his head. "I didn't mean for you to do this. You could get in trouble."

I shrugged. "Maybe. But it's important. And if I don't speak up when it's important, when will I? Right?"

Out of the corner of my eye, I could see the reporters writing down everything we said.

"Hey, Beautiful." Mark sat down next to me and kissed me on the cheek. Flashes went off as I turned to him.

"What are you doing?"

"What, do you think I'm going to let you have all the fun?"

Then, as the reporters continued to yell questions, students started sitting down around us until only the reporters were still standing. The news crew had to back up to get us all into their pictures.

Mr. Thompson laughed out loud. "Now this is what I call a protest."

*　　　*　　　*

By ten, two more news crews had showed up to film for the noon news. Thompson told us all to not answer any questions unless we wanted to. "And you should go back to class. I appreciate the support. Really I do." Thompson held his hand to his chest. "But it's not necessary. This is my fight."

"And we want to help, T."

"Yeah!"

"You rock, T."

Thompson laughed and sat back down. "I guess they want to stay."

Mark grabbed my hand. "This is great. A protest and I get to sit next to the prettiest girl in school."

"Mark. We need to talk."

Mark frowned. "That doesn't sound good."

I looked around. "And this is kind of a terrible place to do this but . . . what was with the boyfriend thing? I thought you didn't want any big commitments."

"It doesn't mean I don't consider you my girlfriend."

I pulled my coat tighter and shoved my hands in my pockets. I felt frozen. A protest should not happen in January. "Mark. Can we back this whole thing up? Maybe be friends for a while."

"You're giving me the 'let's be friends' speech? Are you serious?" He looked hurt.

"It's just things with the two of us always happen so suddenly. We're totally together or totally apart. I'm not saying it to get rid of you. I really think we need to be friends for a while. See if we're right for each other."

"Beka." Mark put his arm around me. "There's no doubt in my mind that we're right for each other. I just want us to be able to enjoy it and not get bogged down with all the drama that comes with being committed."

"You just called me your girlfriend in front of half a dozen reporters. You don't think that was a little dramatic?"

Mark smiled with half his mouth, his cheek dimpling. "Maybe. I just don't want anybody messing with you."

"And I appreciate that. I really do but . . ."

"But?"

"I just don't think we have the same definitions of things."

"What do you mean?"

"Do you really want to get into this? Now?" I jutted my chin toward the huddles of reporters and news crews.

"Why not? What else are we going to do today?"

I pulled some Blistex out of my pocket and put it on my lips, trying to think of what to say. It was so much easier to think of what to say than to actually say it.

"Can I have some?" Mark asked.

I held out the tube to him. He took my hand and leaned in and kissed me on the lips. "Thanks." He rubbed his lips together and smiled.

I rolled my eyes. "See what I mean?"

"Beka. You're not getting rid of me that easily. I did lots of thinking last year, and I realized how stupid it was to get jealous over some rumor. I shouldn't have pushed you away like that. Is that what's still bothering you?"

I shook my head. I was now too confused to sort it out. I watched the news reporters tape their spots for the noon news. Dad didn't usually watch TV until the six o'clock news, so I didn't have to worry about him seeing me. I glanced back over at Mark, who was rubbing his hands on his jeans like he was trying to warm them up.

The conversation shifted when Kenzie, the girl who had outed me as the songwriter to the news lady, came over and sat with us.

"Sorry for skating you like that. I guess I thought it was your fault." She wrapped her arms around her legs. "You're all right," she said, nodding.

"Thanks," I said.

I listened as Kenzie and Mark got into an in-depth discussion about some blog they both read on the Internet. It was just as well. With our conversation derailed, I didn't have anything to say.

*   *   *

Nothing exciting happened until just around lunchtime, when a couple dozen more kids walked out and came to join the protest. I was sure that at least a few of them were only there to get out of class. I wondered if Lori had figured out where I was. Doubtful, since she'd probably just think I was sick, and not freezing my rear off outside. But eventually Mrs. Brynwit stomped out of the building, and we all watched her walk toward us. The cameramen hoisted the cameras on their shoulders and the photographers snapped away.

"You are again disrupting my school."

"It's public property, Eleanor."

She stuck her chin in the air. "Maybe, but I can . . . and will—" she swept her hand at the rest of us sitting around Thompson—"have these students suspended."

I closed my eyes for a second, wondering what I had really gotten myself into.

"You're not going to suspend them. You'd have to take every one of them to the school board for approval. And they'll never approve it."

Mrs. Brynwit glared at him. "We will not have this conversation out here. In front of these children."

Thompson jumped to his feet. "That's just it. They're not children. They're young, maybe even immature at times. But they have a voice and a right to express themselves in appropriate ways." Thompson was growing redder, and he jabbed his finger toward the ground with every point. "I have never, never, allowed a song to be performed that was inappropriate. Just because you disagree with the message doesn't mean it shouldn't be heard."

Mrs. Brynwit tightened her lips into a fat knot but still said nothing. The cameras were capturing everything.

"Very well, then." The words shot out of her mouth like darts. "We will draw up an agreement to . . . ensure the rights of the students . . . and your program." Her face twisted as if the words even tasted bad in her mouth.

"And there will be no consequence for the students?"

"No."

"I'll come right back out here if I don't like the agreement."

"I assumed as much." Mrs. Brynwit walked around all the students and went back to the building.

Thompson clapped his hands together. "That's it then. Thank you kindly for your help. Now back to class."

The crowd groaned, and the cameramen aimed their lenses at us as we stood. I went over to T, who was folding up his blanket. "So that's it? It's over?"

Thompson smiled. "All of you kids, the publicity—I imagine Mrs. Brynwit was forced to concede." Thompson laughed. "She doesn't have many friends left at the school board. I doubt she'll be here next year as it is."

"So why did you do it? Why didn't you just wait till she was gone?"

He looked at me and put his hand on my shoulder. "To be an example to you all, my students. Sometimes you just have to speak up and stop injustice. Even if it's just to protect a couple of performance pieces, it was important. Did you learn something out of all this?"

I nodded.

"Then I did my job, right?"

"You've got a funny way of doing things."

He laughed and we turned toward the building. Mark was standing at the corner waiting for me. One crisis over, another one waiting to explode.

Dad just shook his head when the news recapped my day at school. They didn't say anything about me, didn't even use my name, but they used a clip of me sitting down next to Thompson, and you could see me staring up at Mrs. Brynwit and Thompson when they argued at the end of the protest. I looked older with my hair cut, but it was still odd to see myself on TV.

"How do you get yourself into these situations, Beka? I don't get it," Dad said.

I shrugged and swallowed the bite of Popsicle I had just put in my mouth. "It just seemed like the thing to do."

Dad flicked the TV off, took off his glasses, and turned toward me.

"What? Dad, I'm not even in trouble at school."

"It's about the move. Gabby told me . . . I feel terrible, Beka. Really terrible." He threw up his arms. "I meant to talk to you. I don't know where my head's been."

"It's okay. I get it." I chewed on the Popsicle stick and watched him. It wasn't like my dad to miss a chance to have a major talk like that. "Are things at work that bad?"

"I'm afraid so. But the move. Do you understand? Are you okay with it?"

"I understand. But leaving here . . . even if I'm away at college . . . I don't know. This house is so . . . Mom. You know?"

He nodded, his eyes rimmed with red. "Yes, I know exactly what you're saying but . . . but that's why I think it would be good for me . . . for us. We're all still holding on to her in our own way. We need a fresh start."

"I don't want to forget her." The tears came at the same time as the words. "I feel like I already am."

Dad got to the couch in two strides and dropped down next to me, putting his arm around me. He didn't try to say anything, he just held me.

I closed my eyes and went through the snapshots in my mind again, replaying the scenes I remembered best. I could almost hear her laughing when the border she put up in Anna's room slid off the wall in one long, soggy strip. It was so strange to look back and miss her so much and also remember how unhappy I was at that point in my life. I would give a lot to have that time back with her. I missed out on being with her while I was pouting in my room. So stupid.

Dad leaned back and wiped my cheeks with his hands. "I wish I could make things different for you."

"I know."

*   *   *

I felt better after that and went to bed, determined not to worry about Mark. I had told him what I wanted; it wasn't my problem if he didn't want to listen to me. Right? At least that's how I tried to convince myself.

When I came down for breakfast I was actually looking forward to going back to school. Now that things had settled down and Thompson was going to get his agreement, maybe the rest of the school year would be uneventful. Dad came in and dropped the paper in front of me and my bowl of cereal—Captain Crunch with a ring of Corn Chex.

"You might want to read that." Dad tapped his finger on the paper.

I flipped it open. I was in the picture on the front page, with Mark on my left and Thompson on my right. It would have been fine except for the caption that read, "Becky Madison (center) sits with Roy Thompson and her boyfriend, Mark Floyd." I groaned out loud. I scanned the article, and there was one other mention of me about my song.

"I don't believe they put that in there."

Dad frowned. "The boyfriend thing?"

"Yeah, the boyfriend thing. Guys are just so . . . so . . ."

"Random." Lucy said as she came through the door. She didn't smile, but she seemed to be in a little bit better mood.

"Yeah, so random." I shook my head and looked at the picture. "Oh, no. Oh, no." I dropped my head on the table. Just when I thought things might get back to normal.

"What?" I heard Dad say.

"What if Josh's parents read this? What are they going to think?"

"Just explain it to them. They'll understand." Dad screwed the lid on his coffee cup and put on his jacket.

"Sure. Yeah. I'll just call them up and say 'Don't worry that I was on the front page of the paper with some guy who's not your son saying that I'm his girlfriend.'"

Dad came over and kissed me on the top of my head. "It will be fine. You need to call them anyway to let them know about Seattle."

"Way to share my pain."

He waved and walked out the door with Anna, leaving Lucy and me at the table.

"So my life's a mess. How's yours?" I stirred my cereal, but now it was too soggy to eat.

Lucy shrugged with one shoulder and took a bite of her cereal.

"So the 'not talking' thing. Is this going to be a permanent condition?"

"I just want to forget about it. Can't you get that?"

"Fine. I just want to know you're going to be okay.

And that I'm not going to find you at any more parties with people like Mai Tanigawa."

"Then you can leave me alone. I'm never going to another party. Ever."

I laughed. "Sure. Never's a long time."

*   *   *

Lori leaned on the locker next to mine before homeroom. I was about to spill my troubles with the newspaper photo and then I took another look at her face.

"Everything okay?" I asked. I closed my book bag and slid it over my shoulder.

"Same old stuff. Their counseling session didn't go so well yesterday."

"I'm sorry."

"I just keep hoping he'll figure it out."

"What do you mean?"

"How much he hurt her. That it's really a problem."

"He will. With God, all things are possible, right?"

Lori seemed to be thinking about it, but after a minute she looked up and nodded. "You're right. I can't change anything. God can."

We walked to class and I told her about the photo and my conversation with Mark yesterday.

"But he totally didn't get it. What should I do?"

"It sounds like you'll have to end it. I don't think 'friends' will work with you two."

"Why?"

"Cause you two are so tied up with each other. Anyone can see it."

"Really?" I didn't feel tied up, did I? But I wanted things to change without really letting him go.

As if Mark knew we were talking about him, I felt an arm go around my shoulder. "Hey, Beautiful."

"Hey." I looked at Lori and she lifted her eyebrows at me. "You doing anything after school today? Maybe we can finish talking."

Mark scrunched his eyes up. "Not more talking." He slapped his hand to his chest. "You're killing me with conversation. Let's go do something fun."

I laughed. Maybe I was too tied up, because the last thing I wanted to do was say no. I didn't look at Lori on purpose.

"You can come too," Mark said to Lori. "Let's go bowling. Wear ugly shoes, put the bumper rails up. It'll be fun."

"Can't. I've got dance class tonight."

"And my Beka. Or should I call you Becky?"

"Please don't."

Mark grinned. "So it's a date."

I agreed. At least I could try to talk to him at the bowling alley.

*   *   *

I was proofreading an article during journalism when Mai pulled up a chair across from me. Her eyes were dark slits.

"Dodged another bullet, huh Madison?"

I drew in a deep breath. Ignore or attack? I wished

she would just disappear. Gretchen transferred schools, why couldn't Mai?

"You have your article ready yet?" I asked. I tapped the papers I was reading to straighten them.

"This isn't over."

"Oh, yes it is, Mai. You lost. Deal with it."

Mai laughed, obviously not threatened at all by me. It was kind of humiliating actually. "How's your little sister doing?" she asked.

"Don't even. Lucy is done with you."

"Really? Interesting. And Mark?"

"You've got nothing, Mai. Nothing at all. Why don't you just run along and get your work done."

She lifted her eyebrows and snorted. "I guess you'll just have to wait and see."

I watched her cross the room and settle in at one of the computers. I let out the breath I had been holding. She couldn't do much to Lucy, or Mark. In fact, she might just do me a favor if she scared Mark off. Then I wouldn't have to deal with it.

*   *   *

Mark had already gotten a lane and he waved at me when I went into the bowling alley. I rented some shoes and went and sat next to him to put them on.

He kissed me then covered his mouth. "Sorry. Habit."

"Sure."

He grinned and wrapped his arms around me when I stood up. His smile faded. "What's wrong?"

"You don't listen to me."

"What? About being friends? No. I don't believe that's what you want. It's not what I want."

I moved his hands and picked up a ball. I lined up my shot, took three quick steps and let it sail down the alley. All but one pin fell down.

"You're hot," he said, lifting an eyebrow at me. "In more ways than one."

I spun around and looked at him, at least five feet between us.

"What do you want out of us? Is this just for fun?"

"No. I care about you."

My ball popped up in the return, and I lined up another shot. I watched it fly down the lane and barely miss the pin. Mark picked up another ball and took my hand before I stepped down.

"You don't have to take everything so seriously." He pulled my hand to his mouth and kissed it.

We bowled two games and then went and sat in the snack bar to have a pizza.

During the game I had watched him smile and flirt, and I even had fun. But I couldn't shake the feeling that I shouldn't be there with him. Something just didn't seem right.

Mark sighed as he pushed his plate away. "What can I do to cheer you up?"

"This isn't going to work, Mark." I took a long sip of my Dr. Pepper to watch his reaction.

"It's working just fine. It's only been a week. You owe it more time than that."

"No. I already know. If you don't want to be friends that's fine, I understand."

"Then why did you get back together with me in the first place? Why would you do that?"

"Because I like you. What girl doesn't like to be chased a little bit? Maybe we shouldn't have started dating again. Not so fast."

Mark's lips thinned out, and he looked at the table in front of him for a long minute. Then he stood up and slid into my side of the booth and took both my hands into his.

"Beka, please. Let's give this some more time. You're so good for me. I'll try to be better for you. I'll do whatever I can to prove myself to you."

"I don't want you to have to prove yourself to me." My heart was thudding in my chest.

"But I will. And if you need more from me, I'll give it to you." He let go of my hands and reached behind his neck. "Here. I wanted to give you this." He held up a chain that had a thick, decorated cross hanging from it, something I had seen him wear from the first day I noticed him. He reached around me and fastened it around my neck and whispered in my ear, "When you talked about being friends yesterday, I realized that you were serious and that I couldn't lose you. Not now. It'll just be you and me, okay? I can do that for you." He leaned close and kissed me softly and then gathered my hands up again.

I looked at him, my thoughts flying in every direction. *Just him and me? What does he mean by that?* I leaned closer and he wrapped his arms around me, his hand smoothing my hair. I should have asked.

I stared at my phone for at least half an hour once I got home. I had to call Nancy. I couldn't go to Seattle with her family. I fingered the necklace around my neck and paced around my room. It struck me that even though I hadn't meant to, I had lied to Josh in my letter to him. Well, I had told Mark that I wanted to just be friends. It just didn't work out that way.

What Mark had said was true. We were good together. It could work. It had a better chance than anything working out with Josh. Besides, Josh was really only looking for a deeper friendship with me, at least that's what he said. He knew we couldn't be any more when we were so far apart. Maybe if I had gotten a chance to know him better before he left, things might have been different.

I picked up the phone and dialed the number. I had to get it over with.

Nancy's mom, Terri, answered.

"Ohhhh. Beka." She didn't sound nearly as friendly as she had in church on Sunday. She had to have seen the paper.

"Yeah. I was calling . . . you know . . . about Seattle."

"Oh. Okay."

"Well, I, well I'm not sure it's going to work out for me to go with you. I mean, I'd really like to and all, it's just . . ."

"We understand. That's fine. We expected it really, after seeing your picture in the paper."

"Yeah." I swallowed hard. I couldn't think of anything to say. I couldn't even defend myself. The silence was horrible. "Is Nancy there?"

"Sure. I'll get her for you."

Not that I knew what to say to Nancy either, but it's not like I could just hang up.

"Beka? You're not going?" Nancy asked when she picked up the phone.

"I just think it would be better if . . ."

"Because of that guy in the paper?"

"Sort of. He's not my boyfriend, but I guess we are seeing each other." I was so glad we were on the phone and I didn't have to see her face.

"Oh."

But I didn't need to see her face to hear the disappointment in her voice.

"It's just all kind of complicated right now, and it wouldn't be fair to Josh or you guys to go all the way out there."

"Does Josh know?"

"About Mark? Yeah. He knows." At least he knew most of it. I felt so sick inside.

"Well, if Josh knows about it, then . . . look, I need to go. I'm just upset about all this. I thought you cared about my brother. And to see you with . . . that guy."

"I know. I'm sorry."

"I need to go. Bye." The phone clicked, and I held it in my hand until the monotone voice told me that if I needed to make a call to hang up and try my call again.

I wished that I could. I needed a do-over for the whole day.

*   *   *

I worked on my homework and then got out my Bible. I had been reading it a lot more and had honestly thought I was doing better with learning to listen to God. But instead of making things better, I had made a royal mess. And I still wasn't sure how.

I picked up my guitar and worked out a song.

> I want to hear
> the little voice
> to know what to do
> and which way to turn.
> I need to hear
> the little voice.

My ears seem too big
but I'm trying to learn.

Little voice
speak to me
help me hear
help me see.
Little voice
speak to me
I need to hear
I want to see.

Had I done the right thing with Mark? My feelings felt so jumbled up. Before Mark came along, guys weren't really interested in me, and maybe the only reason I thought I should break up with him was because I was nervous. I didn't want to get hurt. I wasn't always sure what I should and shouldn't do physically. And Josh seemed safer because there would be less pressure. But maybe I was just being immature—trying to run from the pressure. Maybe it was time to learn how to handle a real relationship.

Now that the damage was done, and I had probably killed any chance of Josh anyway, I figured I might as well try to make it work. Besides, I didn't have to try to like Mark. That part was easy.

*   *   *

Mark was waiting at my locker the next morning with a grin on his face. "Hey, Beautiful." He wrapped his arm around me and kissed me on the neck.

"Hey yourself. Is Thompson here? Have you seen him?"

Mark laughed. "Relax. It's going to be fine."

I finished getting my books, closed my locker, and leaned against it. Mark stepped closer. "We should celebrate. Do something special this weekend."

"What are we celebrating?" Dumb question, but I still wanted to hear the answer.

"Us. Now that things are back on track." Mark slid his hand out to the side.

"I'm going out of town on Saturday. Gabby's taking us to some dress shop to get fitted for our bridesmaid dresses."

"Well, I guess it's Friday then." The bell rang and he leaned in and gave me a quick kiss. "Can't wait to see you again."

He turned and I watched him walk down the hall until he turned the corner, then I left in the opposite direction, with an uncontrollable smile spreading across my face.

*   *   *

"So what does this mean exactly?" Lori asked at lunch.

I shrugged. "We're together if that's what you mean." I avoided looking at her and instead glanced over where Mark was eating with some other guys.

"Beka. I thought you said you were going to just be friends with him. What happened?"

"I don't know. He doesn't want to be just friends. And I don't either. Look, it's not like we're getting married or anything. We're dating, having fun. Maybe I could even be a good influence on him. Help him get more serious about God."

Lori shook her head while she drank from her straw.

"What? He believes in God. He's just . . . unfocused." I watched her for a minute as she stared at me. "I thought you liked him now."

"I do like him. I'm just not sure you're thinking very clearly."

I filled Lori in on the Josh situation. "So Josh isn't going to work anyway. I might as well make the most of what I have. Mark likes me, and Josh only wants to be better friends."

Lori sat back in her chair and folded her arms across her chest. "So that's what you think God wants you to do?"

"I don't know what God wants me to do. Everybody has an opinion about it—you, Josh, Mark, even Gabby. It's not just my decision. I can't make things different."

"I know, but what if Josh lived here? Would it be different then?"

I shrugged. "Maybe." I glanced over at Mark again. "But Josh isn't here, and this is our senior year. I don't want to spend it alone."

Lori shook her head again.

It would help a lot if she just agreed with me, especially since I still felt funny about the whole thing. I probably just needed to give it some time.

Mark came over to the table as we were leaving and

draped his arm around my shoulder. We walked down the hallway, and I realized again how Mark always turned heads, and it made me feel good that I had turned his.

It was a relief to get to fifth period and find Thompson there, ready to teach. I wanted to ask if everything had been sorted out, but since it really wasn't any of my business, I just flopped into one of the chairs. He grouped us to work on an assignment, and I was put with Wendy and Tia. I didn't really know either one of them very well, and they were both sophomores.

"So I heard you and Mark Floyd have a thang," Tia said.

I glanced over to T's office, but I couldn't see Mark from where I was sitting. I just lifted my eyebrows.

"He's so cute. Definitely the cutest senior," Wendy said. She and Tia both giggled.

"We better get going. Should we start on the triads?"

Tia and Wendy were easy to work with, and I was glad they seemed to know what they were doing. It took us the rest of the period, but it was exciting to really be able to understand music and composition better. And I even figured out how to fix a part of the song I had worked on the night before. It was like every day I was able to discover a little more about the music, like uncovering little treasures. If I had started earlier, I would have been farther along, but I'd be able to take more music classes in college.

College. It wasn't very far away anymore.

*   *   *

As soon as I walked into journalism, I scanned the room to get a handle on where Mai was and then went to my desk. I picked up a piece of paper that I thought was Ms. Adam's "See To It" list, but this was no list. It was typed, with no signature, but it was obviously from Mai.

You know what I want. You know what I can do.

It had to be the editor's job. I couldn't even think of anything else. But even though I knew that Mai could sway opinions and start rumors, she really didn't have anything on me anymore. What a relief! Lucy was out of her circle for the time being. It was all a lot of huffing and puffing. She really couldn't do much to me that hadn't already been done.

Right?

I tossed the paper aside and decided it was best to just ignore it. Letting it bother me would just make her feel better about herself. I wasn't about to do that.

Ms. Adams and I worked on feature assignments with my assistant, Sabrina. She was turning out to be a huge help, and I figured she'd get the job of editor for her senior year. It would be odd not to be in this school anymore. Everything was going to change.

*　　　*　　　*

Youth group was the last place I thought I would go, but when I realized that Lori and Mark were both busy and that I would have to face Nancy at our Bible study tomorrow, I thought it might be better to face her at church first. I tried to get Lucy to go with me, but she refused to go.

*　　*　　*

Morgan waved when she saw me, her hair bouncing with her steps. Nancy followed her over, but I couldn't read her expression.

"You came," Nancy said.

"Yeah." I kicked at the carpet with one shoe.

Morgan gave me a hug. "Andy Remmick brought three friends with him tonight." She held up three fingers and giggled. "Public school guys, too."

That made me laugh. I remembered that Morgan had been boy-crazy when I met her, and apparently nothing had changed.

"Yeah, well, I see public school guys all the time. They're not that great. Trust me," I said. I rocked back and forth on my heels, avoiding Nancy's eyes.

"It's better than the guys at my school. Total posers." Morgan shook her head and snuck a look behind her. "I'm going to find out their names. Save me a seat."

Morgan bounced off, and I gave a small smile to Nancy. "So."

Nancy rolled her lips in between her teeth, looked at the floor and then back up at me. "Beka. I don't want us to stop being friends over this."

"Me neither. But it feels kind of weird. I can just imagine how I'd feel if it were my brother."

"But you can't make yourself like someone. I guess I thought it was a done deal."

"Me and Josh? But I never . . ."

"Not you. Josh. It just sounded like he was sure about you."

I felt as if I was trying to breathe with someone sitting on my chest. I didn't want to ask, but I did anyway. "Why would you think that?"

"It was just the way he asked about you, talked about you. I've never heard Josh talk about any girl like that."

I had a sudden urge to run away—not just from youth group, but from everything. The pressure was too much. I walked over to a bench nearby and sat down with my knees pulled up to my chest. I put my head down on my knees and closed my eyes. I felt like I had made a horrible mistake.

"Beka. Don't feel bad about it. You can't make yourself like Josh."

But I did like him! Why couldn't he just have gone to school close by? Everything would have been different. This felt so unfair. My friend Celia, who had moved away before my mom died, always complained about not having a boyfriend and how nobody liked her. Lori had one nice boyfriend who adored her, and even though he was away at school, he was within driving distance. Anyone would think it would be a great problem to have, two guys who were both interested. But it felt awful. Like whatever I did, something was going to go terribly wrong. I wanted to grab Nancy and tell her that I wasn't sure about anything and how if circumstances were different . . . but I just sat there, my head too clogged with confusion to even think.

Then I looked up and saw Mai and Liz standing in the foyer of my church.

Nancy looked over her shoulder to where I was staring in utter horror.

"What?" she asked.

"Those two girls. They're from my school."

"Is that bad?"

"Very, very bad."

Nancy sat down next to me and leaned back against the wall. "So are we okay? I mean with each other?"

"Yeah. I'm just so sorry."

"So you really like this guy from your school?"

"Mark? I don't know."

I was still watching Mai and Liz get greeted by a stream of other kids. Now I really wanted to go home.

One of the leaders came out and said they were getting started, and Kathy walked over to where Nancy and I were standing.

"Beka? We kind of have a little issue, and I thought you might be able to help us."

I looked at Nancy, but she shrugged.

"One of our singers from the worship team is sick, and I was wondering if you would fill in for us tonight." Kathy shoved her hands in her jeans pockets.

"But I've never practiced with the team. I'm not sure I can . . ." I said.

"The words to the music are up there for you, and Katie will help you. I'm sure you've heard all the songs. Please?"

Nancy smiled and cocked her head at me.

"I guess I can try," I said. Figures they would ask me when Mai and Liz were here.

I followed Kathy to the stage and David came over with Katie. He showed me the songs and thanked me. He said I could skip anything I wasn't sure of, but as I paged through what they were going to sing, I was glad to see everything looked familiar. I scanned the room and saw that Mai and Liz were standing with Steve, a guy who went to our school. Had he invited them, or did they just show up?

At first it was strange singing in front of everyone, but after the first song I felt more comfortable. It was actually fun being up there with them, and David came over after it was done and invited me to be on the worship team with them. It was very different than performing, but I enjoyed it just as much.

After a while we all sat down, and Kathy and Dan led the session. We ended up in small groups for the last part of the evening. Morgan, Nancy, and I were in the same group with two other girls, Rochelle and Kerri, and our group leader, Leslie. We sat in a small circle in a corner of the sanctuary. We started out by praying, and then Leslie looked around at all of us.

"Okay, scale time. How are you and God doing on a scale of 1 to 10, 1 being 'I don't even remember the last time I talked to Him' to 10 being 'I'm on the verge of rapture'?"

"Do you think we'll be raptured?" Morgan asked.

"So not going there tonight, Morgan. But you start. Where are you at?" Leslie asked.

"Maybe a five. Not great, not awful."

"Eight. Always room to improve," Nancy said.

Morgan rolled her eyes and pushed Nancy's shoulder. "Figures."

"What about you, Rochelle?" Leslie leaned forward, her elbows on her knees. She looked at Rochelle, who was twirling her straight brown hair around her finger. She was pretty and very tan considering it was January.

"Five."

"Me, too," said Kerri. Her hair was as straight as Rochelle's but very blonde.

"Beka?" Leslie asked.

"Five." It was the most popular answer, but it also happened to be true.

"Well that's a lot of fives. How do you think we can move those up to sixes? Any ideas?" Leslie asked.

We spent a while giving a lot of the suggestions I

already assumed, like reading the Bible, praying, listening to God. But they also mentioned things like fellowship, youth group, and coming to church. Other than starting the Bible study with Lori last week, I hadn't been very committed to coming to youth group, or even Sunday school for that matter.

Lori was practically the only person left at school I even talked to, and she was busy with the things going on in her life. Maybe it was at least worth a try.

After the small groups broke up, everyone wandered back into the foyer to eat. I stuck close to Morgan and Nancy and watched Mai and Liz mingle. Mai was putting on such an act. She was smiling and laughing, acting like she was having the time of her life. Liz was quieter, but I figured Mai had made her come anyway. I wanted to walk up to Mai and ask her what she was doing here, and I would have, except I didn't really want to know. All I wanted was for her to just stay away from me.

*　　*　　*

And she did, at least the next day. I was nervous driving to my Bible study, because even though I had broken the ice with Nancy, I felt terrible about the whole thing. I was the first one there, and Lori knew something was wrong the minute I walked in.

"That bad, huh?" she said. I had told her about my conversation with Nancy the night before and how I still felt confused.

I curled up on the sofa after I had hung up my coat and kicked off my shoes. Lori sat down with me.

"It's just all so crazy. There's no perfect answer—at least that I can find." I rubbed my face with my hands. "Please, just tell me. What should I do?"

"What should you do about what?" Megan asked from the doorway.

I looked up and I could feel myself blush. Here she was trying to help us all grow spiritually, and I was having some crisis over a couple of guys.

Megan came and sat down with her coffee while I told her the basics of what was happening. But before we even finished, Nancy and Stephanie showed up. Megan gave me a wink and said, "We'll chat later."

I felt a little relieved. She was a mature woman; she'd know what to do. But as the Bible study dragged on, I became more worried that she'd tell me something I didn't want to hear.

When we finished up, Stephanie was chattering about something with Megan and Lori, and Nancy motioned to me to come over to where she was getting her coat.

"Do you want to come over tomorrow night? You could spend the night maybe," she asked.

"Oh. Well I . . . I actually have plans already."

"Oh." She sounded disappointed. "Maybe another time then."

"Sure," I said. I waved good-bye to her. Everything was so messed up that I didn't even want to be around her anymore. Every time I saw her I thought of Josh, and that wasn't very helpful.

Stephanie finally finished up and left, and we all sat back down again.

"So what exactly is it that you're struggling with?" Megan asked.

"Do you think there's a right answer? About who I should be with? I'm seventeen. Should it be this complicated?"

Megan smiled. "So you don't think you made the right decision? To date Mark instead of pursuing something with Josh?"

"I don't know. It's just easier with Mark. I know exactly where I stand with him."

"And Josh is in Seattle," Lori said.

"Exactly." I lifted my hand in the air.

"Do you love Mark?" Megan asked.

"He says he loves me," I said.

"That's not what I asked."

"I don't know. I don't know if I trust him enough to really love him. But I don't know Josh very well either. I just don't think I'll ever be good enough for Josh."

Megan sighed and leaned forward on her knees. "I'd love to just give you some sort of answer. But I can't. I don't know what's right for you, or what plan God has for you. But this I do know—God is in you, and He'll tell you what you need to know if you're willing to listen."

I felt deflated. We talked for a while longer and then I had to leave for my counseling appointment. I talked to Julie about it as well, and she said practically the same thing Megan had said. Adults were always saying kids never listen to them, and here I was ready to listen and no one would give me an answer.

I went home and prayed for a while and asked God for help. I needed Him to come through for me. I needed an answer—or at least to feel like I wasn't floating in the wrong direction.

Then my phone rang.

I grabbed it before the caller ID flashed. "Hello."

"Beka?" I wasn't sure of the voice.

"Yes?"

"It's Josh."

I dropped onto the edge of my bed. I instantly felt nervous and fluttery as if he could know what I was thinking.

"Oh. Josh. I wasn't expecting . . . hi."

"Hi." He paused for a second. Should I say something? Before I could say anything he continued. "I got your letter and I've been trying to write back but . . . I just couldn't seem to get the words right. I wanted to call so we could actually talk."

"Okay." The slight flutters in my stomach turned into a tornado, and I was being sucked down into it. I was just plain old embarrassed. Instead of just writing back, he decides to call. Great.

"I don't even know where to start," he said. "First off, I don't care if you're seeing Mark."

"What?"

"It doesn't matter."

"But . . ."

"It doesn't. Beka, when I left to come back to school, we didn't have any commitments. We didn't make any promises."

"I know. But it still felt like maybe . . ."

". . . something was going on between us?" he finished.

"Yeah. I guess. I just feel awful about it."

"Please don't. You have nothing to feel bad about. And I don't want you to feel pressure from me either. The only one you need to worry about pleasing is God."

The words stung even though I was sure they weren't meant that way. Was I pleasing God in anything I did?

He continued. "Beka, I still want to get to know you. You fascinate me. I just want us to go slow, really become friends."

I wanted to ask him if he thought we might be more than friends, if it was really going somewhere, but I couldn't get the question out of my mouth. So I asked the other one.

"How, though? How can this work?"

"A country apart? I just think it will. It actually might be better this way. Being physically close may make it hard for us to really hear what God thinks."

"Why's that?"

"Well, I'm not tempted to lean over and kiss you right now."

So he did think about kissing me?

"Yeah, I guess that wouldn't work too well." I forced a small laugh as I swallowed the lump in my throat.

"Now, about this other thing you said in your letter. About me being able to do a lot better than you? Did you mean that?"

"Yes." I twirled the phone cord around my finger and closed my eyes.

I heard him sigh deeply. "You have no clue how wonderful you are, do you?"

Was I supposed to answer that?

He continued, "Beka, just because you're new at following God doesn't mean I don't see what God is doing in you. That's why I want you and me to keep moving forward."

"Josh, it's just . . . well, I bet there are girls falling all over themselves to get your attention out there. You're like this perfect guy or something."

Josh laughed out loud. "Beka, I think I need to tell you a story, about what kind of guy I really am. Maybe then you'll understand."

I curled up on my bed and pulled a blanket over myself. "Okay."

"You know Nancy and I were adopted. But I was almost ten when my parents adopted me. My dad—my birth father—was a drug addict and a dealer, and when he was high he'd beat my mom. Dad stayed away from me because Mom would always throw herself between us and she'd take it for both of us. It's all I had ever known. By the time I was eight, I could steal and shoot a gun—the only things my dad ever taught me to do. It was right after I turned nine I couldn't take it anymore. It was like watching my mother die right in front of me. So one night I stole his entire stash and emptied it out onto the ground. I sprayed it with a hose until there was nothing but mud left."

"What happened?"

"Dad came home with a couple of customers, and when he came inside to get their stuff he went wild. He grabbed my mother and accused her of stealing it. He wouldn't stop beating her. I tried to get him to stop, but he threw me against a wall. I landed halfway behind the couch. When I got to my knees I saw my dad's gun taped to the back of it, just in case one of his deals went bad. It all happened so fast. I pulled the tape off the gun and stood up, pointing it right at him. My mother was bleeding, not moving, and my dad just turned and looked at me. He laughed and said, 'You ain't gonna use that.' He swung his leg back and kicked my mom in the head, and I squeezed the trigger three times. Two went into the wall, but one went into his belly."

"Oh, Josh."

"I panicked and went to call for help. The ambulance came and got them both and took me to a foster home."

"Were they okay?"

"My mom lived for a couple of weeks but her head . . ." Josh's voice cracked and I felt my own nose burning. How could all that happen to a nine-year-old boy?

"What about your dad?"

"He was fine, but they arrested him and he went to prison, for the drugs and for what he did to my mom. He's still there."

"Do you ever see him?"

"No. I know it's probably something I'm going to have to deal with someday. I think I've forgiven him, you know, and then I'll realize that part of me is still angry with him."

"Oh, Josh." It's all I could think of to say.

"I spent seven months in foster care before going to live with the Crawfords. They had already adopted Nancy, so I was number two."

"I thought you knew her when she was little. Like calling her Jelly Bean."

"Dad called her that, I just picked it up, listened to all the stories. I've heard them so much I sometimes have to remind myself I wasn't actually there."

"I had no idea. I'm so sorry."

"So I have plenty of my own baggage, including a convict father that I shot. Does that shatter your image of me as some perfect guy?"

I thought about it. "No. It makes it even worse. That you could go through all that and still be who you are . . ."

"But that was all God. Believe me, it took a long while for me to get to the point where I really trusted God. I was angry and hurt and blamed Him for everything being so messed up. But He was faithful to me. That's why I can be so sure for you. I've seen what He can do, firsthand, and I want to be a part of your life, to watch and see what He'll do with you. And us."

"I don't know what to say."

"Don't say anything. Just think about it. Would it be okay if I called you again?"

"Sure." We said good-bye and I dropped the phone back on the cradle. I couldn't even move, so I just lay in my bed and closed my eyes.

What are You doing, God?

By the time Friday night rolled around I had finally made a decision about my Mark/Josh dilemma that I felt good about. I wasn't even sure how except to think that God really had answered me. The answer was just sort of there—totally obvious even though I had never seen it before. It made me feel better, but I wasn't sure exactly how Mark would react to it.

His little Celica pulled into the driveway right at five. I had gotten a new burgundy shirt with a bow in the center that hung down. I loved it and I felt good.

He got out of the car and opened my door. When he went to kiss me, I turned enough to let him catch me on the cheek. He didn't say anything until he had gotten back into the driver's side.

"Now how about a real hello?" Mark leaned over to me. I wished he had just let it go because I didn't really want to have to talk about it right away.

"I said hello already. So where are we going?"

Mark frowned but sat back up and pulled out of the driveway. "I thought we'd go to The Rock Garden and then maybe to a party."

"A party?"

"Just to have some fun. Besides, it's at Shane's house and I said I'd drop by. You don't mind, do you?"

"I guess not. Is it a drinking party?"

Mark laughed. "Remember that first party I saw you at? You were so trashed."

"I'm not like that anymore." I watched the lights flash by outside my window. The memories of that time weren't good.

"You know I don't drink. We'll just hang out and have fun."

"I also remember back then that you didn't want me going to any of those parties. So why are you all into them now?"

"You've been dragging me to them to get your sister. I only want to go to this one because of Shane."

I supposed he was just trying to be a good friend. At least that's what I told myself. All through dinner he talked about how he had these plans to start a band in college and how his parents were upset about him wanting to go to Tech instead of Berean or Liberty.

I listened but it was weird somehow. I couldn't put

my finger on why I wasn't really enjoying myself. I was with the cutest guy in the senior class. I refocused on him, watching his cheek dimple as he talked, and tried to listen as we drove out to Shane's house.

I didn't know Shane very well, but Mark had introduced us a couple of times. I knew he had worked as a techie on *Annie*, but other than that I didn't really know much about him. The party wasn't quite as huge and throbbing as some of the others, but I still worried about seeing Mai there. At least I wouldn't be chasing after Lucy.

Mark managed to find us some sodas, and he found us a spot in the living room. I felt like I was just a painting on the wall watching everything happen around me. Mark had his arm around me, but I didn't have anything to add to the conversation. Finally I got too bored to sit there anymore.

I leaned close to Mark and told him I'd be right back. He nodded and I went looking for a bathroom. Every room was filled with kids now, many of whom I didn't even know. I locked myself in the bathroom and pulled the clip out of my hair. It was giving me a headache— well, it was either that or the music. I checked my face, and when I felt like I couldn't stall any longer I wandered back out into the party. I saw Liz in the kitchen, by herself. I had to find out.

"Hey Liz."

"Beka." She smiled but her eyes darted around. I wondered if she was looking to see where Mai was. "I'm surprised you're here."

"So am I. Mark wanted to come."

"I always come." She took a drink from a plastic cup and rubbed her tongue along her teeth.

"So you came to my church the other night."

"Yeah. It was nice."

I almost laughed. "What were you guys doing there?"

"Oh. We went with Steve."

"I figured. But why?"

Liz took another drink. "I better get back. See ya." She smiled and walked away.

Liz acting nervous and fidgety was nothing new, but it made me even more curious about why they were there. I considered going to ask Mai. If she were drinking then maybe she'd end up telling me the truth.

I found the door to the basement and went down. It was just a large unfinished basement with a pool table in the center, some rugs scattered around, and some beat-up old couches. There was a group playing pool and some others gathered around the couches. I saw Mai standing by the back door with a small group, including Liz and Jeremy. I didn't want to confront her when she was with people. I hung back and pretended to watch the pool game while I really watched Mai.

I felt two arms go around my waist. It didn't even occur to me that it wasn't Mark, but when I turned my head, it was Shane. I twisted around so his hands came off of me.

"Want to play?" He stepped close and I could smell the beer on his breath.

I took a step back and shook my head. "No. I'm just watching." I turned back toward the pool table, but Shane stepped up next to me. He draped his arm over my

138

shoulder and whispered in my ear, "Want to get out of here for a while?"

He was inches from my lips when I realized he was actually going to try and kiss me, but I ducked down and spun out from under his arm.

"Gross. I thought Mark was your friend."

Shane shrugged and stumbled toward me again, obviously undeterred. He smiled. "Playin' hard to get, huh? Thas' all right with me." He reached toward me as I backed away and grabbed my belt loop. By this point we had a small audience, and I just wanted to get out of there. I took his hand and pulled it away from my jeans and shoved him with my other hand. He laughed.

"Feisty little thing."

I bolted up the stairs and found Mark exactly where I had left him, only now Angela was sitting in my spot with her arm around Mark. And Mark didn't seem to care.

I walked over and lifted my eyebrows when he looked at me. He patted his lap. "Sit here." Angela slid her arm away but didn't move. I held up my watch and mouthed, "Can we go?"

Mark frowned and mouthed, "What's wrong?" to me.

I shook my head.

As soon as we got outside the door, Mark grabbed my elbow.

"What's wrong with you tonight?"

"I'm not going to any more of these things. Everybody just acts so stupid."

"What's wrong?"

"Your friend Shane, that's what's wrong. He tried to grope me in the basement."

Mark drew his eyebrows together for a moment and then laughed. "Shane? He's harmless."

"Did you hear me? He tried to kiss me and grab at me."

"Beka, he didn't know what he was doing. He won't even remember it tomorrow."

"I will." I pulled away from Mark and stood by the passenger side door.

He unlocked the doors and I yanked mine open. He drove me home in silence. I guess I expected him to get mad, defend my honor, something. He got out of the car with me once he stopped in my driveway, and he caught me in front of the car, the headlights streaming behind both of us.

He wrapped one arm around my waist and lifted my chin with the other.

"What's wrong, Beautiful?"

"I already told you."

"Beka, he didn't mean anything by it." Mark moved to kiss me and I turned away. "Why won't you let me kiss you? You've been dodging me all night." He tried again and this time I dropped my head so he kissed me on the forehead. He blew out a frustrated sigh.

"I thought we agreed to take it slow. You said you wouldn't push."

Mark reacted in surprise. "Yeah, but we weren't talking about kissing. Come on." He pulled me close and kissed me. I let him for a minute and then pulled away, my heart racing.

"I just want to go slow."

"We are."

"Not slow enough. Can't we cool the kissing, for a little while? I just need time to get used to this."

"Why do you want to go backwards? I want to kiss my own girlfriend."

The streetlights behind him were casting a shadow across half of his face. I couldn't tell if he was hurt or angry. But I stood my ground. It was the first decision I felt really good about. Mark searched my face and then let go of me.

"Good night, then." And with that he climbed back into the car and backed out of the driveway. I stood there for at least ten minutes, wondering not if I had done the right thing, but why it had taken me so long to see it.

It was too late to call Lori, but I really wanted to talk to her.

*　　*　　*

Gabby had wanted Lucy, Anna, and me ready by seven in the morning to go shopping for dresses. All three of us were Gabby's bridesmaids, and Paul was going to be my dad's best man. While Gabby was wrestling with Anna's braids, I followed Lucy out to the SUV. Lucy climbed into the last seat in the back, and I slid into the middle seat. We sat for a few minutes in total silence before I decided to go ahead and ask her.

I turned sideways so I could see her. "So. How are you?"

Lucy wrinkled her nose. "I'm going back to sleep." She pulled a blanket off the floor and used it as a pillow.

"I just thought maybe you wanted to talk about Ethan."

"I don't want to ever hear his name again."

"Oh. I thought . . ."

"You and everybody else." Lucy didn't open her eyes.

"Lucy. That night. It just seemed like . . . well, something happened. Right?"

"I'm not talking about this." She pulled her blanket up to her nose.

Anna and Gabby came down the porch stairs chattering and got in the car. It didn't seem to matter, though, since Lucy obviously wasn't going to talk.

"Why do we have to go so early?" I asked Gabby as she started the car.

"It's going to take two and a half hours to get there, with no traffic. And it's Saturday, so we could hit traffic."

"But don't they sell dresses in Bragg County?" Anna asked.

Gabby laughed. "My friend from college owns this little dress shop. She'd be devastated if I went anywhere else for my wedding. She's been waiting a long time to see me get married."

I tried to read, but it made me feel carsick, so I just watched the trees on the interstate fly by. Gabby and Anna were talking about horses again. Anna had jumped up and down when she heard we were moving out to the farm. Lucy hadn't reacted at all, but I couldn't tell if that was because of her mood lately or because of the actual news. It still made me sick to think about it.

I leaned my forehead on the cold window. There was nothing interesting to look at. So much had already changed since my mom died, and now the biggest change of all was coming. Would I be able to seriously stand up there and watch my dad pledge his love to someone else? I looked at the back of Gabby's head. There was no doubt she was happy, and I knew she loved Dad. I had known that even before they started dating. Anna was going to be fine. I wasn't so sure about Lucy. Or even me.

I had imagined some tiny little dress shop in the back of someone's house, but Gabby pulled up in front of a large beautiful storefront with "Sweet Caroline's" written across the windows. We climbed out of the car, Lucy yawning and Anna bouncing up and down saying she had to go to the bathroom. The door of the dress shop flew open and a woman with shoulder-length platinum-blonde hair came running out.

"Gabby! You're finally here!" I assumed that this was Caroline. She had a thick Southern accent, and she squeezed Gabby until I thought she'd pop.

She clapped her hands together and sucked in her breath. "And who are these gorgeous girls?" She slapped her hand on her chest. "These can't be the Madison girls. Gabby, they're gorgeous!"

Gabby introduced each of us, and Caroline grabbed each of us into one of her death hugs. I was last.

"I still have to go to the bathroom," Anna said.

"Mercy me, let's get you inside then. We're going to have a blast. I cleared my schedule, so I'm all yours." Caroline linked arms with Gabby, and we went inside where one half of the room was bright with color and the other half shone with white. After Anna had taken care of things, Caroline led us back to some couches and sat down with some books to get an idea of what style bridesmaid dresses Gabby was looking for.

I wandered through the dress racks, looking first at the bridesmaid dresses and then at the prom dresses. These were so much prettier than typical department store dresses. I almost laughed when I saw the prices. No wonder they were nicer. It made me think of going to prom with Josh last year. Dancing with him and playing games at the house later that night with Lori and Paul and their dates. I got this pang in my chest. I really missed Josh.

I pulled out a deep purple dress and held it up to myself in front of the mirror. The bodice was fitted and sequined and the A-line skirt had see-through silk layered over it.

"Try it on."

I turned to see Caroline watching me.

"Oh. No. It's okay." I walked back and hung it up, but Caroline snatched it back off the rack. "You might as well, we've got a stack already in there for you to model for us." Caroline whisked the dress into a dressing room and shooed me in.

"Now you try that purple one on first, then we'll go through the others."

I slipped the gown off the hanger and tried it on. It was beautiful and it felt so light. I pulled my hair up and spun around.

"Let's see it, Beka," Gabby called.

I came out and blushed when Caroline and Gabby gasped. "It's like it was made for you," Caroline said. "Gabby, she has to get that for her prom."

Gabby nodded, but I held up my hand.

"I don't even know if I'm going to prom. I ended up leaving last year."

I rushed back in and pulled on the next dress for them to see. Each time I came out, Gabby and Caroline walked around me and debated the pros and cons of each style. Once they had narrowed down the style, Anna and Lucy tried some on too. After a few more hours, Gabby had finally settled on a dusty rose-colored capped-sleeve dress. It had a gathered bustline with a knot in the center. It was pretty and I was glad she had nixed Caroline's suggestion of the green "Gone with the Wind" dress that was as big as the dressing room. This one was simple and tasteful.

We had lunch with Caroline and then piled into the SUV to drive back home. Gabby asked me to sit up front, and I reluctantly climbed into the front seat.

"So you like the dress?"

"Yes. I really do." I had only told her a dozen times.

"So tell me about prom. Why do you think you won't go?"

"I don't know. The dancing and stuff last year was raunchy, and we didn't even stay for the whole thing. Besides, I'm just not sure."

"What's going on with Mark?"

I glanced at her, but she was watching the road. I didn't know if I even wanted to talk to her about it. I fingered Mark's necklace.

"We're going out."

"And Josh?"

"We're friends." She didn't say anything, and I felt

this urge to defend myself. "I'm just taking it all real slow. I mean, I don't even know where I'm going to be in the fall anyway."

"That's true."

Then Gabby's cell phone rang. And everything suddenly changed.

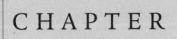
Hey! How are you?" Gabby looked over at me and whispered, "It's Tony."

I nodded and turned to look out the window, glad the conversation was off of Mark and Josh. I heard Gabby getting very excited next to me, saying "Uh-huh," "yeah," and "really?" over and over. After about ten minutes she flipped the phone closed and said, "You are not going to believe this."

"What?" I shifted back in my seat so I could see her better. My mouth went dry. She sounded excited, but when Tony had taken my demo CD out to L.A. with him, I never really expected anything to come of it. But she was obviously excited about something.

"What's going on? I can't hear anything back here," Anna yelled from the backseat. Lucy was sound asleep again on the middle seat.

"Tony wants you to fly out to L.A. on Monday to meet with the producers. We'll stay with him and Carlita. They want to meet you." Gabby sounded like an excited little kid.

"So what does that mean?"

"Well." Her tone turned more businesslike. "They haven't made any decisions yet, but they liked the CD enough to have you come out. It's not just the music they have to consider, but you."

"What do you mean?" I asked.

"Tony said that when they sell albums, they're selling the singer. They need to meet you to get a feel for how they could package you."

Package me? How do you package a person?

"I thought Tony said this would take a long time. I didn't think . . ." I said.

"It usually does, but Tony said they had a development deal go south this week and they've been scrambling to get something in the works. When Tony said you might be available, the producers wanted to have you flown out immediately. That's why it's all so quick."

"So, you would take me?"

"Yeah. I haven't been to L.A. to see Tony and Carlita for a couple of years. It'll be fun. I'm going to need to see if Tracy can cover lessons for me, and Ron's going to have to supervise the building. Oh, and I need to call your dad. Excuse me." Gabby flipped her phone back open and started making phone calls. Gabby gave me a thumbs up after she talked to my dad, so after that I turned and stared out the window again. I felt like I had swallowed lead. It was all happening too fast.

*　　　*　　　*

As soon as we walked in the door I went to my room to call Lori. I filled her in on my L.A. trip first, and she was excited.

"I can't believe it. You have to call me and tell me everything. Not when you get home, while you're out there. You promise?"

"Yes, yes, I promise. And I think I got an answer from God about my Mark and Josh dilemma."

"Really?"

"Well, I told you about talking to Josh and how that made me feel all weird about going out with Mark even though Josh didn't have a problem with it? Well, I realized the other night that the reason it made me feel weird was because of the physical stuff—the kissing mostly. It was a total 'duh' moment. If I didn't do anything physical with Mark, then I could see where it goes without feeling guilty about Josh."

"Okay."

"Don't you see how huge this is? It's like a real answer from God. It makes total sense."

"What does Mark think about it?"

"Oh, well that part may not be going so good. He kissed me once last night before I tried to explain it all to him. But I know it's the right thing to do." I didn't fill her in on my run-in with Shane because it kind of made

149

Mark look bad, and I didn't want to give out any ammunition against him.

"I'm happy for you. Really."

We talked for a little while longer, and then as soon as I hung up with Lori I dialed Josh's number.

"Hello?"

"Josh?" I swallowed hard.

"Beka? Hey, I just put a letter in the mail to you today."

I told him about my trip to L.A.

"Beka, that is amazing. I know God has got great plans for you. But it stinks that you're going to be all the way out here on the West Coast and I won't be able to see you."

"I know. So how are things out there?"

We talked for more than an hour when I realized that it was after midnight and that my dad wouldn't be happy about me still being on the phone.

"Before you go. Have you thought any more about our conversation the other day?"

"A lot. And yes, I do want us to become better friends. I still feel kind of bad about Mark though."

"I told you that you don't have to. I trust God to lead both of us. And you need to be sure that you're making the right choice. As long as we're honest with each other, I think it's the best way to go. For now."

"So, in the interest of being honest. Are there any girls that you're . . ."

Josh laughed. "Nope. Not a one."

My breath caught in my throat, and I had to take a long breath. I was so glad to hear that. We said good-bye and I curled up and dreamed of what Seattle would be like.

*   *   *

Sunday was a mad rush of getting laundry and packing done, and Monday morning we were at the airport.

Dad hugged Gabby and me good-bye, and it caught me off guard to see them kiss each other. Why couldn't I get used to that? They held on to each other for such a long moment that I had to turn away and pretend to be checking the zipper on my carry-on.

The plane ride was a lot longer than I expected, but because of the time difference, it was only 11:00 a.m. in California when it felt more like it should be after two. We had to take a shuttle to the car rental place and then wait in line forever. The weather was absolutely beautiful, and as soon as we pulled into the street I pushed the button to roll down the window.

"I could get used to this," I said.

We drove up the 405 to West Hollywood so we could park on Melrose and find something to eat. The street was littered with funky little clothing shops, and there were more places to get something pierced than I could count. But I nearly died when I saw the Fred Segel store.

"We have to go in there," I said, pointing to the ivy-covered building. "I heard that real stars shop there."

Gabby laughed but let me drag her in. We ordered some smoothies in a small food area, and then we browsed around while I kept my eyes peeled for movie stars. I was so glad Gabby didn't look like she just walked off the farm, which of course she had. She played it cool and pointed to the outrageous price tags.

"That totally looks like Jennifer Garner. Do you think it's really her?" I asked, sucking in my breath.

"Who?" Gabby asked.

"*Alias? 13 Going On 30?* Don't you have a television out there?"

"Yeah, I just never get to watch it. Which one?"

I used my chin to gesture over to where the tall brunette was looking through some tops. She picked out a fancy little spaghetti-strap top and held it out, pursing her lips. It looked like her. I couldn't believe she was so close. I so wanted to say hi, but I also didn't want to look like a total dork. She didn't end up buying the top.

We didn't see anybody else, and since we were due at Tony and Carlita's for dinner we got back on the road. They lived up in Beverly Hills, and we drove up some narrow, twisty roads until Gabby pulled through a set of black iron gates onto a cement driveway. The house was brick but didn't seem very big—until we walked inside.

A housekeeper greeted us in Spanish at the door and ushered us into a grand foyer with a curved staircase that swept upwards. The floors looked like marble and it just looked so luxurious. Carlita appeared at the top of the stairs looking like she was making a movie entrance. Her thick dark hair and olive skin were perfectly made up, and she wore a silk top over a pair of jeans.

"*Bienvenido!* I'm so glad you made it." When she reached the foyer she nodded at the housekeeper and said, "*Gracias,* Yelena." The housekeeper scurried off and Carlita opened her arms to hug Gabby. "We finally have you back in L.A." She turned to me. "And Beka. Welcome. Let me show you two around."

Carlita gave us a tour of the house. The house went on forever, and every time I thought there couldn't be any more rooms, she'd show us another one. Gabby and I had a suite where we each had a bedroom and shared a bathroom in between. From my window I could only see trees and some other houses dotting the hillside. But when Carlita took us out on the patio off the kitchen we had a spectacular view of L.A. I leaned on the stone wall and just stared. The sky was just beginning to turn pink. I could hardly believe I was standing there. School and Mai and home seemed so far away.

"Beautiful, no?"

"Yes. I've never seen anything like it. Thanks for having us."

"It's our pleasure." She put her arm around my shoulder and squeezed. "We'll be family soon."

Family. I never imagined that Gabby becoming part of my life would lead me here to this spot. No matter what happened at the meeting tomorrow, I was determined to enjoy myself.

"We must go to meet Tony. Go ahead and freshen up, all right?"

I nodded and went back to my room. I dragged my suitcase onto the bed. All of my clothes seemed hopelessly East Coast, so I opted for a T-shirt with a tank top layered over it and a flared skirt. It was the best I could do. Maybe Gabby would take me shopping in the morning before I had to go to the studio. As soon as I thought about it, the butterflies kicked up in my stomach.

Carlita drove us in her BMW. I sank into the leather seat in the back and rolled down my window enough to get some fresh air but not so much to destroy my hair. Carlita pulled up in front of a place called Spago's, and the valet whisked the car away. Tony was waiting at the entrance, and when he saw Gabby he grabbed her in a hug and swung her around.

"You're here!" He set her down and then gave me a hug. "There's my girl. We have lots to talk about tonight." Tony turned to kiss Carlita and took her arm, leading us all into the restaurant. Everything seemed to be wood and marble, and they led us to a table on the edge of the patio where we had a view of the one-hundred-year-old olive trees that the maître d' pointed out to us. Even the fanciest and most expensive Bragg County restaurant couldn't compare to this. I just didn't want to look like some backwoods hick.

Tony and Carlita helped us order, and once we had our drinks Tony lifted his glass and said, "To family."

"To family," we all echoed and clinked our glasses.

Tony took a long drink and then rubbed his hands together. "Here's where we stand, and why I wanted you to get out here as quickly as possible."

Carlita laid her hand on Tony's arm. "Business? So soon? Should we catch up a bit first?"

"It's fine, Carlita. I'm sure Beka would like to hear. We'll have time," Gabby said.

Tony looked around to see if everyone agreed before he continued again. "We've had a development deal fall through, and Seth was very interested when I gave him your demo after Christmas."

"Excuse me—Seth?"

"Sorry. He's one of our A&R guys. They are the ones who try to find new talent to sign. So Seth wanted to bring you out here to put you in the studio, meet the marketing and publicity team."

"That sounds like a lot of people."

"I'm afraid there's even more. We'll take some pictures of you in the morning . . ."

"But I don't have any good clothes to wear," I said. I looked over at Gabby. I hated getting my picture taken.

"I promise. It will be painless. We have a wardrobe. And I took the liberty of inviting Sylvia Marks to join us for lunch. She's a manager, and even though I can vouch for the integrity of the studio, it's in your best interest to have your own manager."

I looked around the table. Carlita was calmly sipping her water, and Gabby looked just as bewildered as I felt.

"Tony." Gabby leaned forward. "We don't have to pay for a manager, do we?"

"No, no, no. She only makes money if you do. It all works on commission. She's a personal friend of ours and is doing this as a favor, since you don't have a deal yet."

The rest of the conversation was a complete blur. I tried to listen, but they were batting around so many new words and concepts that I felt like I'd have to take a class to understand them all. Only when they mentioned UCLA did I tune back into the conversation.

"What was that?" I asked. I took a bite of a warm roll from the basket, hoping it would settle my stomach.

"We have a tour scheduled of Asuza Pacific on Wednesday morning and UCLA in the afternoon, so you can get a look at the campus," Carlita said. "Don't worry. It will be fun."

"I don't understand." I squeezed the roll in my hand and looked around the table.

Carlita's voice was calm and even. "If you need to move here to work in the studio, wouldn't you like to continue to go to school?"

"I . . . I . . . I guess but . . . I thought this was all some long shot. You all are talking like this might actually happen." I laughed. "You're not serious, are you?" I looked at each of them and instead of finding amused looks on their faces, they were watching me closely as if they didn't understand *me.*

I pulled my hands into my lap and straightened my shoulders. "Are you serious?"

Tony wiped his mouth with his napkin and reached over and put one hand on my shoulder. "We'll see what happens tomorrow but . . . it all looks good."

I didn't sleep all night. I had called my dad after dinner, but instead of being shocked by what I told him, he seemed to already know. Which completely confused me, because even though it had sounded exciting when Tony first mentioned the possibility, I had never let myself think that I would even get this far. I got into the shower hoping that it would wake me up. Now that it was morning, I was finally ready to sleep.

We all climbed into Tony's Hummer, which had to be the coolest car I had ever ridden in, only I wasn't able to enjoy it very much. Gabby sat next to me and asked if I was all right, but all I could do was shrug.

The studio didn't look all that exciting. It was just a large kind of nondescript building, but inside it was warm and inviting with lots of wood and color. Tony walked us right past the receptionist and took us to the elevators. We went up to the fifth floor where we went down a hallway and into a large room that was set up as a studio. Tony walked in and shook hands with a large bearded man wearing a salmon-colored shirt.

"This is Beka. Beka, this is Gren." Tony gestured toward me and I lifted my hand.

"She is small." Gren rubbed his beard and walked around me in a circle. "Hair is good." He bent over and put himself nose to nose with me. "Skin is good."

Tony laughed. "Don't worry, Beka. Gren will take good care of you. I'll be back for you. Call me when you're finished with her."

"Yes, yes." Gren waved Tony away, and Tony kissed Carlita and disappeared through the door. "Come," Gren said to me. "We get started."

Carlita and Gabby stayed for a while, but after an hour Susie and Lynn were still doing my hair and makeup, so they told me they were going down to get some coffee. Once they finished, they led me into a wardrobe room where they chose some pieces for Gren to look at. He picked out several tops, skirts, and pants and told them which ones to start with.

The first outfit made me feel like a fashion model. The material was silky and feminine but not immodest. I looked at myself in the mirror for several minutes, not even believing that it was really me. They had layered my hair even more and teased it so it stood out from my head all the way around. The makeup was dramatic and totally unlike anything I had ever worn. It almost felt like I was wearing a costume.

"Is she ready? Where is she? Ahhh." Gren came around the curtain and held his hands apart. "Here she is. Yes. Yes. This is good. Susie. The hair here. A little up, no?" They played with my hair more and walked around me in circles, moving me around like a puppet. Carlita and Gabby came back in chatting, but stopped and stared when they saw me.

"Beka? It hardly even looks like you," Gabby said.

"Amazing," Carlita agreed.

Gren finally seemed satisfied and moved me in front of the cameras, where he took at least a hundred pictures in all sorts of different positions. I had to smile, laugh, and be completely serious in every one of the outfits I changed into. At one point he had me lying on my belly underneath a piano bench, which I thought was strange since I didn't even play the piano. It felt awkward, but it was fun once I got used to everybody watching me.

Gren finally seemed to have everything he wanted, and I noticed Tony standing in the doorway watching, sipping out of a stainless steel coffee mug. Carlita and Gabby went over to him, and when I came back from changing they were still there talking.

"How did it go? Do you feel like a star?" Tony asked.

I felt myself blush. I nodded.

"Well, our big meeting isn't until two, so we're going to have lunch with Sylvia, let her get to know you a bit. How does that sound?"

And we were off again.

*　　*　　*

"So you're the future niece I've heard so much about." Sylvia held out her hand and I shook it. "Tony lent me your demo. Loved it."

"Thanks." We all settled in at an outdoor table at the little bistro we had walked to. Tony and Carlita did some catching up with Sylvia before they turned their attention back to me. Which was fine because I needed some time to get my legs under me. I felt like I was in way over my head. Sylvia scared me a little at first because she was kind of abrupt and outspoken, but after a while I could see that it was just her way. I imagined it made her a good manager. But I sort of felt like I was on trial once she started asking me questions.

"How much music training have you had?"

"What is your primary style of music?"

"Where did you learn about composition?"

"How much music have you written?"

"Where do you see yourself musically in five years? Ten years?"

I felt like an idiot because the answers I did know made me feel backwards, and the ones I didn't made me feel like such a novice. I actually started feeling really stupid about being there at all until she finally stopped and closed her notebook and leaned back in her chair. I was sure she was going to scold Tony for wasting her time with some East Coast girl who had barely even started learning about real music and composition. I chewed on my bottom lip and swore that I wasn't going to cry, no matter what she said.

"Well, Tony, she's young and inexperienced but you know, you may just have something here. She's got a unique sound, and she's not like the scads of pop princesses that come through here every day of the week. She's got some depth, and if she can translate that to her music, you just may have something."

"So you'll come to our meeting?" Tony asked.

"Absolutely. Let's see what we're dealing with."

I leaned over to Carlita. "What just happened?"

"You just got yourself a manager." She put her arm around me and squeezed.

*   *   *

We all walked back to the studio, Tony and Sylvia rambling on about stuff I didn't understand, and Gabby and Carlita talking about the beautiful California weather. I hung back trying to take it all in. I wished I could have some time by myself to think, to pray. I felt like I had been put on a train and I couldn't get off now if I tried. It was moving too fast.

We went straight to the A&R meeting, as Tony called it. At the door Tony shook hands with a guy who didn't look that much older than me. He had dark blond hair and was dressed in a sports jacket and button-down shirt, but instead of a tie, the collar was just open and casual. Everything in California seemed casual. He held out his hand when Tony introduced him to me.

"Beka. This is Seth Waller. He's going to be running the meeting." Tony held his hand to his chest. "Seth is the one I told you about that is interested in signing you."

I tried to smile, but I think I was clenching my teeth. I was so worried about how screwed up my face must have looked that I tripped over my own feet and crashed right into him.

"That's not the usual greeting I get." Seth lifted me by the elbows and held on. "You got it?"

"Yeah." I adjusted the straps on my shoes to give me an extra minute before I stood back up. Seth was grinning.

"Don't worry about it, okay? It can only help a guy's ego to have a pretty girl fall all over him."

Tony slapped his arm around Seth's shoulder and pointed a finger at him. "That's my niece you're looking at, boy. Remember, I'm still your boss."

Seth winked at me and cleared his throat. "After you, Tony."

Seth took my arm and led me into an enormous conference room. It was mostly men, but a few women were scattered among the group. He leaned over and whispered to me, "Now I'm going to introduce you and talk about what we'd like to do, and then they'll have a chance to ask you any questions they might have. After that, you'll go on out with Tony and then I'll work my magic on them."

"Who are all these people?"

"Mostly it's A&R. They're sort of the talent scouts, but there are also people from marketing and promotion. We need to have everybody excited when we sign a new artist, because that's the only way CDs sell."

I tried to swallow the lump in my throat as Seth settled me into a big black chair and the meeting got started.

Seth introduced me and told them about me and where I had come from. He explained to them why he thought that even though my inexperience made me risky, it also made me fresh and different. After that it was a total blur. All sorts of people began firing questions, and when I didn't answer fast enough, Sylvia, Tony, or Seth would jump in and give an answer. The room seemed to have less and less air in it, and even though there was water on the table, there was no way I was going to be able to reach it. I would have had to lay flat on my stomach, and even then it would have been a stretch. Finally, Seth walked me out into the hallway to where Gabby and Carlita were waiting for me.

Seth patted me on the shoulder. "You did great. We'll catch up later." He turned and rushed back in.

I shook my head. "I don't know what that meeting was, but that was awful."

"What happened?" Gabby asked, clutching her hands together.

"I don't know." I let them lead me down the hallway into Tony's office. I sank into an oversized chair, kicked off my shoes, and curled up. "Except for Seth and Tony, I don't think any of those people think I deserve to be here."

"Tony says these meetings are always hard. It's about money and if you're the one they want to invest that money in."

I shook my head. "What happens now?"

"We wait."

I stared out the office windows, but all I could see was the blue sky and some thin wispy clouds drifting by. It didn't seem real that I was here, that all this was happening. I loved to sing, surely that was something God had put in me. But is this what I was supposed to do with it? I could see myself teaching music in some elementary school, but recording CDs and touring—I had never even imagined. Just because a door is thrown open, did that mean you had to walk through it?

We waited for an hour before Tony, Seth, and Sylvia came in. I sat up and slipped my shoes back on, figuring there wouldn't be any decision to make anyway. Tony perched on the edge of his desk while Seth stood next to him and Sylvia settled into the last empty chair.

"Well, Beka," he started.

Yep. It sounded like bad news. At least I could go home and focus on graduation, college.

"We've still got some kinks to work out, but it looks like we're moving toward a deal. I'll have to talk with your dad, of course, but it looks good. Real good."

"What would that mean for me exactly?" I spun the bracelet on my wrist in slow circles.

"You would move here and live with Carlita and me. You could still go to school, but you'd need to take a light load while we're recording the album."

"I've only written a couple of songs. I don't know if I . . ."

"Don't worry about that. We have a number of talented songwriters that we work with. We may pair you up with existing material, or we could have you work with somebody on some composition for new songs. Those are all details we can work out later. But what do you think? Are you ready to move to L.A.?" Tony watched me, probably sensing my confusion.

I shot Gabby a look, and she rescued me. "Tony, this is a lot to take in. Let's talk to Greg and see what he thinks and give Beka few days to think about it. Is that okay?"

"Absolutely," Seth said. "We want everybody to be happy with the arrangements. We'll work with Sylvia on the contracts on this end, and all Beka needs to do is talk with her family and decide what she wants to do."

Everybody started talking at once, and I felt like I was being pulled backwards through a tunnel. Everybody seemed small and faraway. I dropped my head down and tried to run my fingers through my hair, but with all the teasing and the hair spray, I got the bracelet on my wrist hopelessly tangled up in my hair. I sat up slowly, my hand stuck to the back of my head.

"Excuse me." I stood up and walked out, trying to make it look natural to walk with my hand on the back of my head. Carlita followed me out into the hall.

"What happened here?" She reached for my wrist and worked to get it free. "This is a lot, no?"

"Yeah. I guess I didn't really think anything would happen."

I felt the bracelet fall from my wrist, and I was able to let my arm down, but the bracelet was still in my hair.

"Many, many girls dream of being where you are today. Nothing is by accident. Tony hears many singers and bands. He tells me some have talent and some have passion. Very few have passion and talent. When he saw you at Christmas, he says he sees both in you." Carlita held my bracelet in front of me. I held out my hand and she piled it into my palm. "You should not say yes

165

because of the opportunity. You should only say yes if that is what Jesus says in your heart." Carlita tapped her own chest. "He will tell you what you should do. Trust Him." Carlita wrapped her arms around me and squeezed.

The next day Carlita and Gabby and
I went to tour first Asuza Pacific and then UCLA. I got a
chance to talk with admission directors at both campuses.
The UCLA campus was enormous, like an entire city, but
after an hour and a half of walking around, it didn't
seem quite so overwhelming. There were even areas with
grass and trees, something I wasn't necessarily expecting.
I picked up an application for late admission, figuring it
would be better to have it in case I decided to come to
L.A.

It was still strange to even think about it. I hadn't
called home yet, not even to talk to Lori. Part of me
wanted to call everybody I knew and see what they

thought I should do. But it was going to end up being my decision. I was the one who was going to have to live with it for the rest of my life. After the tour was over and we had eaten lunch, I asked Gabby and Carlita if I could walk around by myself for a while. The tour guide had showed us Bruin Walk, a spot on campus where students walked between classes and mingled with each other, so I found a nice spot to sit and watch people walk by.

There were so many people, more nationalities than I had seen in a lifetime in my small town. I tried to picture myself there, book bag over my shoulder, on my own. It would be a leap just going away to college, and coming here would be like leaping whole galaxies away from everything I had known. I didn't want anything to change, yet everything I knew was scattering away. I was powerless to stop it. I closed my eyes and then opened them again, taking it all in. I needed to hear from God. Inside I felt so torn. What an amazing chance I had, something few people ever got a shot at. And yet a part of me wanted to feel safe and comfortable, stick with what I knew, with what everybody else was doing.

God, I need You like I've never needed You before. I don't know what to do. What do You want me to do? Everybody tells me You really do have a plan. I need to know what that is, what that looks like for me. Help me to hear You.

*   *   *

We arrived back home at night, but it still felt like the middle of the day to me. Dad came and got us from the airport and took Gabby straight back out to the farm. When we were alone in the car, Dad cleared his throat.

"So Butterfly, what did you think?"

I turned in my seat a little and rested my face against the leather. "I just don't know. It's like I watched it all happen to someone else in some movie. It doesn't seem real."

"Taking Paul to college last year was hard, but you . . ." Dad was quiet for a few minutes. "No matter where you go next year it will be hard to not have you here. To say good-bye."

"I wish it never had to change. Not that I want to stay in high school, but it just feels like everything I'm used to is going to disappear."

"I know what you mean. Tony filled me in on all the logistics, but I want to hear what's on your mind."

I looked at my dad's strong silhouette and felt just like I did when I was little and scared; I would go and crawl into his lap and tuck my head underneath his chin. Nothing could hurt me there, I was sure. But then things had happened that even my dad couldn't stop, and that had made me wonder if there really were any safe places. He was still strong, but not in the same superhuman way I used to think. He was just a man, who was starting a new chapter of his life with a new woman. Where did that leave me? His new chapter wasn't my new chapter. I wasn't sure I was ready for our paths to split apart so soon. I still felt like I was just a kid.

"I don't know, Daddy. I guess I'm realizing that I have to stop trying to go backwards."

"What do you mean?"

"Trying to keep everything familiar, the same. It's not ever going to be the same again. I mean I knew that, but going to L.A., it would be really hard."

"It could be really wonderful too."

"What do you think Mom would say? If she were here?"

I saw Dad smile sadly. "I think she'd tell you to spread your wings. That it's time for you to fly."

"What about you?"

Dad turned the car into the driveway and put it into park, but made no move to get out. "The Dad side of me wants to keep you here, tucked away in your room. L.A.'s a big city and you're my little girl. I don't care how old you are, that's how I'll always see you. It would be different if you were going to live there by yourself, then I think I'd have some issues with it. But you won't be alone. I know Tony and Carlita would watch out for you."

"So you think I should go?"

"Butterfly, I'm with you either way. Is it what you want?"

I just didn't know.

*   *   *

As soon as I got to my room I felt really guilty about not calling Lori. I had even promised I would. I listened to messages from Lori and Mark for at least fifteen minutes, and by the last one from Mark, I wasn't too eager to call him back. He sounded mad. Lori would understand though, so I called her first.

After begging her to forgive me for not calling her, I told Lori in detail everything that happened in L.A. I lost count of how many times she said, "No way!"

"What would you do if you were me?" I said when I was finished.

"This is so amazing. I can't believe I know you."

"Lori. It's just plain old me, remember?"

"Yeah, but Beka, this is one of those life-altering things, you know. Promise me you won't forget me?"

"I don't even know if I'll go yet."

"You'll go. You have to go."

"Whose life is this anyway? It certainly can't be mine."

"Oh, and I had to tell Mark where you were."

"I figured. I've got six messages from him. I guess he's upset I didn't call him."

"I guess you better go call him then."

I stalled after Lori and I got off the phone because I couldn't come up with a good reason why I didn't call him. I just hadn't even thought about it.

I ended up going to bed instead.

*   *   *

Going back to school on Monday was bizarre. Everybody else was the same, and I just felt so different. Like I had been through some experience that no one else could really understand. Mark was waiting at the front doors, but he wasn't smiling. I took a deep breath and walked toward him.

"Hey, you," I said, smiling as if nothing was wrong.

"Why? Why wouldn't you call me?"

I kicked my shoe on the ground and looked back up at him. "I don't know. It felt weird. Like I would have been bragging or something. Besides, it all happened so fast."

Mark took my face in his hands and pulled me close to him. "I would have been happy for you. Why would you leave me out like that?"

I felt so rotten. All I could do was shrug.

He moved closer and kissed me. I didn't have the heart to push him away either, since I had already hurt his feelings.

He put his arm around my shoulder and we walked into the school. "Promise me you'll let me in, Beka. We're together, right? I should be part of these things."

"You're right. I'm sorry." But even as I said it I had never felt farther away from him.

I struggled the rest of the day, trying to sort out why I felt so strange being back at school. I had a ton of work to catch up on, and my desk in journalism looked like someone had dumped everything they could on top of it. Sabrina had handled last week's edition of the paper, so I tried to sort out what was current and what could be put aside. Somewhere in the middle of the pile I found a sealed envelope with my name typed on the front.

I slid my finger in the envelope and pulled out a piece of paper, double-sided, and a smaller slip of paper with "Last chance. By Friday." typed on it. I knew it was from Mai of course, and usually I'd get all tense and nervous, but I didn't this time. I looked at the double-sided paper and noticed it was typed and arranged in columns as if it were a newspaper. The title read "The Truth" and the lead headline read, "Banker Under Scrutiny" and another, smaller one read, "Are You on the Wrong Path?" I skimmed through both articles. The banker article accused several bankers of pointing fingers at one another for a substantial amount of missing funds, and the wrong path article was basically telling everyone they needed to get Jesus or they were headed to hell. The words were rude and angry.

I flipped it over and found small paragraphs under a title that read, "What's Going On?" I recognized several names, but when I saw Lucy's I dropped into my chair. It said, "Even my own sister Lucy is not immune to the ravages of sin in the earth. Since discovered doing the nasty with Ethan Sardon, I can only pray for her very soul." I only read a couple more before throwing the paper down in disgust. They were tidbits of gossip under the guise of pointing out other people's sin. And Lucy? I felt sick. I put my head in my hands. Was Mai going to copy that thing? And pass it out?

And she made it sound like I was the one who wrote it.

I folded it up and shoved it in my backpack when I saw Ms. Adams headed for my desk.

"Everything okay?" she asked, pulling up a chair to my desk. She leaned her elbows on the table and adjusted her glasses.

"I'm fine." I scanned the desk and found the "See To It" list she had left for me.

She looked at me as if she was trying to decide whether to believe me. I wanted to ask for help, but what could she really do? I couldn't prove who it was, and what if I made it worse if I got other people involved?

"All right. I'm so glad to have you back. You ready to go over the layout?" She spread out the proof sheets and we talked over some changes. But I could barely pay attention. All I could seem to think about was Mai, who was watching me from the bank of computers on the far wall.

*　　*　　*

It wasn't until I got home and read through "The Truth" that I realized what the banker article meant. Even though no names were used, she had to be talking about my father. Dad said there were problems at the bank. Could the article actually be true?

I wandered downstairs after I had finished some of my homework and found Dad staring at his laptop in the den. I sat on the corner of the couch, pulled my legs up, and leaned on the arm so I could see him better.

"Hey Dad."

He didn't move his eyes from the screen. "Hey Butterfly."

"Can I ask you something?"

"Sure, sweetie." He moved the mouse and clicked, then took a breath and turned to me. "Is it about your L.A. decision?"

"The trouble at the bank. What exactly is going on?"

Dad cleared his throat and rocked back in his chair. "It's nothing you need to worry about, sweetie."

"I know. But I still want to know. If Paul were here you'd tell him. Wouldn't you?"

Dad rocked and stared at the laptop. After a few minutes he turned the chair toward me. "Someone has been embezzling money from the bank."

"Embezzling? You mean stealing?"

"Yes, stealing."

My heart pounded in my chest. How would Mai know that? "Go on."

"I think I know who it is, but I have to prove it. Until I do, all the executives at the bank are suspects."

"You, too?"

"Yes, me too." He looked sad. He reached over and closed his laptop.

"But it will be okay, right? You'll find out who did it, right?"

"I hope so. Beka, honey, I don't want you to worry about this, okay?"

"Is there anyone named Tanigawa who works at the bank?"

"Tanigawa?" Dad shook his head. "I don't think so. But I don't know everybody either. Why?"

"No reason. You're not going to, you know, lose your job or anything, are you?"

Dad looked away and started to gather all of his papers.

"Dad?"

He stopped and looked at me. "To tell you the truth, I've been thinking about a career change. The corporate world . . ." He ran his fingers through his hair. "I just think it might be time for a change."

"Because of the money? What's happening at the bank?"

"No. I've been thinking about it for a while. With moving out to the farm, it seemed like a good time."

"Are you serious? What are you gonna do, muck stalls with Gabby? Is that really what you want?"

A smile spread across his face. "It just might be."

I went to my room with my head spinning. I didn't know what bothered me more, Mai being right or the image of my dad wearing flannel working on Gabby's farm.

And if Mai was right about my dad, was she right about Lucy, too?

*　　*　　*

Lori looked at me over the top of "The Truth" and shook her head. "She's got a lot of nerve, doesn't she?"

"So what would you do?"

Lori handed the paper back to me. "She wants the editor's job?"

"Yeah. But I don't want to quit."

"I don't think you should. Have you tried talking to her?"

I laughed. "You're kidding, right?"

"I'm serious. It couldn't hurt."

I thought about Lori's suggestion all day. Why was I scared of Mai? *Pray for your enemies*—I remembered feeling that way when I was having problems with Gretchen. I needed to start praying for her. Talking to her was another story.

But I did keep coming back to the fact that high school was all going to end. A few more months and we'd all go our own separate ways. None of it seemed to matter that much anymore. I still didn't want to quit. I felt like I owed Ms. Adams for giving me a chance in the first place. But maybe there was another way to solve the problem.

Even though her little threat gave me till Friday, I wanted to get it over with. Mai was sitting at a table talking with Liz. I watched them until I saw Liz get up, leaving Mai sitting there by herself. I walked over and sat down across from her. She glanced up and scowled when she saw it was me.

"What do you want?"

"To talk." She was just a person. Right?

She snorted.

"Mai. What is it you want?"

She glanced around and lifted her eyebrows. "Don't be stupid."

"That's not what I'm talking about. What did I ever do to you?"

Mai dropped the paper she was holding, leaned back, and crossed her arms across her chest. "Little Miss Perfect. Just doesn't know what to do when things don't go her way."

"This is a joke, right? Do you seriously think everything goes my way?"

Mai pinched her lips together and stared at me for a long minute. Then she burst forward and slapped her hands flat on the table. "How dare you," she growled at me. "I can't go anywhere without you being in my face. It's my turn."

"Your turn for what?"

"First Gretchen and now you. I won't be second place anymore."

"Why do you think you're second place?"

Mai just glared and shook her head. "C'mon. You're smarter than that, Madison."

"I can't believe you'd want it this way."

"You only got that job because Ms. Adams felt sorry for you."

"No, I didn't."

"Puh-lease."

"Why does it matter anyway? The year's almost over."

She didn't say anything, but I thought I saw something that looked like fear cross her face. I didn't know what she could possibly be scared of, but I had an idea on how to solve the problem. If she'd go for it.

"Look, you'll probably never have to see me again

after this year. And I don't know why you're so upset with me. But why don't we compromise? I'm not going to quit. That wouldn't be fair to Ms. Adams. But what if we shared the job?"

Mai turned her head a little and looked at me from the corner of her eye. "What do you mean?"

"Coeditors. I think Ms. Adams would agree to it. Especially since the special senior edition is going to take so much work."

"Coeditors? I could still say I was editor of the newspaper?"

"Yeah."

Mai shrugged with one shoulder. "Fine."

"Fine? You mean that's okay with you?"

"You'll do it now?"

"I can talk to Ms. Adams today."

"Go ahead, then." She picked her paper back up and I left, smiling as I walked away. Could it have been that easy? Was it over?

Ms. Adams was fine with the change, asking if I was sure I wanted to share the job. I had my doubts about how well it would actually work, but I was willing to try anything. I hadn't mentioned "The Truth," and neither had Mai. I could only hope that would be the end of it.

*   *   *

After that, life settled into somewhat of a routine at school. Mark and I were still together, but it was almost like we just didn't know what else to do. The incident with Shane had long been pushed aside, but I wasn't surprised when Mark confronted me right before spring break.

We had taken a picnic to the beach because the weather had finally turned nice. It was still cool, so I wore a jacket, but I thought the day had been good. We talked about school and all the graduation activities coming up. But then Mark made a move to kiss me, and I pushed him away. That was all it took.

"Come on, Beka. What's wrong now?" Mark sat up.

"Nothing. Why?"

"We've been dating for months, and I've laid off about the kissing and stuff just like you asked. It's time, don't you think?"

"For what? I thought things were going okay."

"They are." He scooted closer. "I just think we're ready to go to the next level."

I looked at Mark's eyes, obvious with their intent. "I like things the way they are."

Mark took my hand and brought it to his mouth and kissed it. "I do too. But Beka, you can't expect me to be an altar boy forever." He scooted closer. "I'll be a good boy, I promise." He batted his eyes at me and snuck close for a quick kiss.

I had figured Mark was a little frustrated with our arrangement, but I felt so much better about it. It was like the best of both worlds. I was still able to be with him, but I didn't feel guilty about it.

"Mark. I like you. I just don't know that it's smart to change things. I feel so good right now."

"You've changed. Since you came back from your trip. Am I not good enough for you? Is that what it is?"

"No. No. We talked about this before I left. You agreed."

"Yeah, but Beka, it's like we're just friends who hang out. You won't even let me kiss you. And it's not even just the physical stuff. You've changed."

Mark stood up and brushed the sand off his jeans and walked toward the water. I watched him shove his hands in his pockets and look out at the water. Was it fair to keep things going with him? I liked being with him, but I knew it wasn't going to last once we left school. I knew I was being totally selfish, but I wanted to finish the year with a boyfriend. To have someone to go with to graduation parties and the prom.

I walked down and wrapped my arms around him from behind and rested my head on his back. I felt his hands on mine, and he pulled me around him. The wind was blowing softly, and he reached over and brushed the hair out of my eyes.

"I'm sorry. I really am, Mark."

"Me, too."

"You're a good guy. And I want you to be happy."

"But?"

"But I don't think I'm the girl for you. You're not happy with the way things are and I am." I reached behind my neck and unsnapped his necklace.

"It's not that I'm unhappy."

"So where does that leave us?"

"We can still be friends," he said.

"Friends? I thought you weren't interested in being friends." I held the necklace up and dropped it into his palm. He stared at it.

"It's not my first choice," he said.

I stepped closer and let him hug me. We were just having a normal date and now we were breaking up. It seemed so anticlimactic.

Mark drove me home and waved good-bye, but even as he pulled out of the driveway it seemed like I had given up too easily. If I was honest though, we had been heading toward breaking up for a while, but I didn't think it was because I had changed. If anything I thought he had changed.

I walked up to my room feeling sadder than I expected. When I walked by Lucy's door I heard what sounded like crying. Lucy and I hadn't talked much since that night of the party, but since I was the big sister, I knocked on the door anyway. It got very quiet.

"What?"

"It's me. Can I come in?"

"Go away!" she yelled.

Something about how angry she sounded made me try the door handle. Nothing had happened between us to make her mad at me—at least I couldn't think of anything.

It was unlocked. I opened the door a crack and peeked in. Lucy was laying flat on her bed, her face in a pillow.

"Lucy?"

She threw her head up, her face pink and blotchy from the tears. I stepped in and pulled the door shut behind me.

"What's wrong?" I went toward her and then stopped.

"Are you deaf? Go away." She took ragged breaths like she had been sobbing.

"What happened?" I didn't move any closer, but I didn't want to leave either.

Lucy dropped her face back into the pillow and her slender body shook from the sobs. After a minute or so she gave no sign of letting up, so I sat down next to her and rubbed her back. I could feel the muscles tense underneath my hand, but after a few minutes they relaxed and she continued to cry softly.

I didn't know what to do.

I prayed for her under my breath and kept rubbing her back until her breathing seemed to slow. It was almost thirty minutes later before she rolled a little to her side to look at me.

"What can I do?"

"Nothing. You can't do anything." Fresh tears fell down her cheeks and she laid her arm across her forehead.

I looked around for some tissues and then went and snagged the whole box from her dresser. "Here." I pulled a couple out and handed them to her.

"It can't be that bad," I teased.

"It's so much worse."

"Tell me. Please?"

I wanted to know. I wanted to help her. But nothing could have prepared me for what came out of her mouth.

"I think I'm pregnant."

I sucked in a long breath as my mind flipped through the last couple of months.

"Ethan? You . . ." I couldn't finish the thought.

Her face crumpled up as she nodded and began to sob again.

"Oh Lucy." I couldn't think of anything else to say.

She cried for a while longer, and while she did I tried to figure out a plan. But it wasn't until I already had her dressed in maternity clothes that I realized we just needed to take it one step at a time.

"Why do you think you're pregnant?"

"I missed my period."

"When was it due?"

Lucy drew her eyebrows together. "Why?"

"Well, it could be lots of things. Being stressed out can even make you miss your period."

"But we didn't use any . . . oh, this is awful. Dad's going to kill me."

I tried to not think about my little sister with some guy. I wished Paul were here to go wring the kid's neck. But I needed to deal with Lucy.

"You stay here. I'll go buy a test, okay? Let's just take it and see, okay?"

Lucy nodded, and wiped at her eyes.

I drove to the pharmacy and found a two-pack of easy-read pregnancy tests, and I was back home in less than fifteen minutes. Lucy hadn't moved, so I sat down next to her and tore open the package. She sat up. I raced through the directions.

"Okay, this is easy. Let's go."

"What, right now? Here at home?" Her eyes were wide and scared.

"Where do you want to go?"

"I don't know. But what if it's . . ."

"Lucy, let's just take the test and see."

"It was just that one stupid night. I didn't even want to."

I was halfway to the door. "What?"

"I told him I didn't want to do it. He said it was too late."

I walked back to the bed slowly. "Lucy. Did he force you to have sex?"

Lucy's face crumpled up again and she began crying again.

"Lucy." I sat back down. "Tell me what happened. From the beginning."

It took her a while to calm back down, but eventually she told me what happened. "We were just supposed to fool around a little. But he wouldn't stop. He said he couldn't stop."

"Oh Lucy. We have to tell someone about this."

"No. No, no, no, no." She shook her head hard.

"But Lucy, honey. That's rape. He can't get away with that."

"But I went up there with him. It's my fault." She began to sob again.

I shook my head, trying to take in everything. "Look, let's just take this test. See what we're dealing with, okay?"

She nodded and let me pull her off the bed and into the bathroom. I unwrapped the package and showed her what to do, then turned around to give her some privacy.

"Okay." I took the stick from her, capped it, and put it on the sink. "We have to wait two minutes." Lucy and I stood and stared at the stick.

She looked at me after one minute. "Beka? Do you hate me?" Her chin quivered.

I put my arm around her. "I could never hate you. Why would you think that?"

"I messed up. Worse than I ever have in my whole life."

"Lucy. I don't hate you, and God doesn't hate you. Yes, you messed up. But that's why Jesus came in the first place—He knew we were going to mess up."

I picked up the stick after another minute had passed, and there was no line in the round window. I smiled at her. "See, no line. You're not pregnant."

"Are you sure? Really, really sure?" She picked up the stick and shook it.

I showed her the directions. "See. This is what it would look like if you were pregnant. You're okay."

Lucy looked between the paper and the stick several times before she looked back at me. She sighed. "I was so scared."

I hugged her.

"But my period. Why did I miss it?"

I shrugged. "Who knows? Maybe you were stressed out about it."

Lucy sat down on the side of the tub.

"But Lucy. We should still tell someone what Ethan did."

Lucy shook her head again. "No. It's over. I just want to forget about it."

"I understand that, but what if he does it to someone else? He could, you know."

Lucy stood up and pulled her sleeves down. I followed her into her room, where she curled into a ball again. I sat down on the edge of the bed.

"I understand how you feel, but I don't know a lot about this stuff." I looked around her room. It was still a pale blue from when it used to be Paul's. "I'll make you a deal. I won't say anything if you convince Dad you want to go to counseling. I've gone for long enough to know that you can't just pretend it never happened."

Lucy stared at the wall in front of her.

"So what do you think?"

"Would I have to tell him?" she asked.

"That's up to you. He probably won't ask a lot of questions about why you want to go anyway."

She was quiet for a while but then said, "Okay. I'll go."

I felt a weight lift off my shoulders. I knew when I was in over my head, and I figured Julie would know just what to say.

Dad didn't ask a lot of questions, and I drove Lucy to her appointment Monday after school. I was just going to wait for her, but I was surprised when she asked me to come in with her. I smiled at Julie and sat on the couch next to Lucy.

"So what brings you here to see me, Lucy?" Julie asked.

Lucy had her arms wrapped around her stomach and was staring at the floor. She sat like that for several minutes.

"Why don't you tell her what happened?" I said.

Lucy shook her head and then burst into tears. Julie held out a box of tissues, and I tore a few out and pressed them into Lucy's hand.

Eventually, Lucy told her what happened, with a bit more detail than she had clued me into. I felt sick to my stomach thinking that with all my plans to go to that party, I still hadn't protected her. And Ethan was just a fourteen-year-old kid. What was he going to be like at seventeen?

"You're going to need to see a doctor, Lucy," Julie said.

"Why? I'm not pregnant. We checked." Lucy looked at me and I nodded my head.

"But there are over thirty sexually transmitted diseases you can get from unprotected sex."

Lucy started crying again. I didn't think she'd have any tears left, but they kept streaming down her face.

"I didn't want this to happen. I've ruined everything. Absolutely everything."

Julie knelt in front of Lucy and took her hands. "No, you haven't. You made a mistake in judgment. But we'll take this one step at a time."

"I've ruined things with God, too," Lucy whispered. "I'm all messed up now."

"Lucy. Listen to me. No matter what has happened, you are not too messed up. God still loves you. He does. I know it doesn't feel like that right now, but there is nothing we can do to make God stop loving us."

"Am I going to have to tell my dad?"

"Not today. We'll talk about it though, okay?"

Lucy nodded, and by the time our hour was over, Lucy was at least calm. And she was talking, which was good. It made me feel better that Lucy now had someone who could support her and help her make good decisions about how to face it all. She had been going to school with this guy for weeks and was just holding it all in. Now she had a place to let it out.

*   *   *

With Lucy's crisis I had barely had a chance to think much about breaking up with Mark, which was why going to school Tuesday morning was such a huge shock. Before I had even taken my coat off I saw Mark with his arm draped around Angela Byer's shoulder. I was so stunned that I ended up standing in the middle of the hallway like a deer in the highway until Lori grabbed my elbow and dragged me down the hall.

I couldn't even make words come out. I just pointed at Mark and Angela with little croaking noises coming out of my mouth.

"Beka. Are you okay?"

Mark looked over and caught my eye. Without saying anything I just shook my head at him. He looked away and then whispered something in Angela's ear. She turned and kissed him on the mouth.

I swallowed hard and turned away. I couldn't watch anymore.

"Beka?"

"It's only been a couple of days. How could he already be with her? This is so unfair."

"You said you felt it was the right thing to do."

"Yeah, I know." So why did my heart feel like it was full of tiny shards of glass?

"And that you thought you had been drifting apart anyway."

"Yeah, I know." I turned back around in time to see Mark and Angela walk away. "I can tell he's really broken up over it."

I went through the day in a haze and saw Mark and Angela at least three more times. In theory class, Tia and Wendy were asking me what happened with Mark, and it took everything I had not to make Mark sound like a monster. I ended up just telling them we had broken up. I kept looking for him through Thompson's office window, but he never came out. What would I say to him anyway?

When the bell rang I took my time gathering my papers, and when I walked by the office Mark walked out and right into me.

"Hey, Beka."

"Mark."

"Well, I have to go get these copied." He held up a stack of papers.

I shrugged. "Go ahead." *Ask him. Say something.* Mark started out the door.

"Mark?" By this point the room had emptied out, leaving just the two of us. He turned back and waited. "Angela?"

Mark shrugged. "She likes me."

But why so soon? How could you be with her already? Don't you even miss me? The questions only formed in my head. Maybe it was good that I couldn't ask them.

"I better go," Mark said.

I waved as he walked out the door, and I headed

straight for a bathroom. I knew I was going to start crying.

*   *   *

When Mark and I had talked at the beach I wasn't surprised, I had even half expected it. But seeing him with Angela hurt, a lot more than I had thought it would. Part of me felt like fighting for him. Throwing myself at him and asking for another chance. And I was angry with myself for giving up on it so easily. How did I know where things would go in the fall?

I dragged myself home and flipped through the contract paperwork that Tony and his company had sent. Sylvia had worked out all the details, and lawyers had been over it. All that was left to do was sign it and send it back, and I would officially have a recording contract. I still had a couple of weeks to make the decision. While I was sitting there reading it, Dad walked in the back door, smiling.

I hadn't seen him smile like that in months.

"Butterfly! Isn't it a beautiful day?"

I looked at him like I didn't know who he was.

"Looking over your contract? So what do you think you'll do?"

"Dad? What's wrong?"

"Wrong? Nothing. Everything's great. The embezzlement case was settled, and I resigned my job today. Things couldn't be better."

"You quit?"

"Not quit, really. I'm taking an early retirement."

"When?"

"Let's put it this way, when you graduate, I'll be done too."

"And you're happy? I mean, that's what you want to do?"

Dad sighed. "Yes. I told you, didn't I, that I felt like I was done with the corporate world. I'm ready for a fresh start." He sat down in the chair next to me. "This way I'll be around more for Lucy and Anna."

"I think that would be good."

"We're going to have to start packing soon." His tone turned serious. "How are you feeling about the move?"

I held up the papers. "If I sign these I'll be moving to L.A. in August."

"I know, but even when you visited, you wouldn't be coming back here."

"I think maybe you're right. I think we need a fresh start. It will be good for Lucy and Anna. It's not like we can just stay here forever."

Dad smiled and hugged me. "So are you going to L.A.?"

I shrugged. "Maybe. I don't know."

"Well, I'm here if you want to talk." Dad jumped up. "I'm going to start boxing up the garage."

"Today?" I asked.

"Why not?" he said.

I heard him whistling as he walked up to his room. I pushed the papers aside and went to my own room. I was glad my dad seemed happier, but I couldn't shake my own sadness. After dinner I talked Lucy into going to youth group with me. She was reluctant, but I reminded her of some of the things Julie had told her, and she finally agreed.

*   *   *

Even though everyone was friendly and the worship time was good, I still couldn't shake my mood. I just felt sad all over. I wasn't sure if it was Mark, the move, L.A., or maybe it was all of it. Nancy came over with a water bottle in her hand during a break.

"You okay tonight? You seem out of it."

I shrugged. "Just feeling crummy." I took a drink from my own water bottle. "Mark and I broke up."

Nancy raised her eyebrows. "Really? You know, Josh talked to me about that a couple of times. Promised me that he knew what he was doing. Guess he knew what he was talking about."

"Maybe. So I guess you're going out there next week?"

Nancy shook her head. "No, Dad had some work thing he had to take care of, so we decided not to go."

"Oh, I'm sorry. I know you really wanted to go."

"I did. What about you? Have you decided about L.A.? I still can't believe you got offered a contract."

"I know. It just feels like I should be more excited about it or something, but I'm not. The whole idea of moving out there kind of scares me. I never saw myself living very far from home, and now I'm thinking about moving across the country. It seems so crazy."

"Sometimes that's just the way God works."

I hoped she was right. But that was the part that was

bothering me most of all—was this really God at work? I noticed Lucy hovering in a corner, so I said good-bye to Nancy and walked toward her, but just before I got there one of the adult leaders went over to her and started talking. I watched for a few minutes in case she left, but the two of them sat down on the floor and kept talking. I was relieved but felt heaviness in my heart at the same time.

On the way home, Lucy said she was glad that she had gone. I went straight to my room and curled up on my bed. I tried to pray, but I wasn't even sure what to pray for. I didn't know what would make me feel better.

*   *   *

Maybe I just got worse at hiding how I was feeling, because it felt like everybody was bugging me to talk to them. I didn't like being at school, because I couldn't go anywhere without running into Angela and Mark, and home wasn't much better because Dad was boxing things up and making everything look different. I was glad to have spring break come, but knew that Dad was expecting me to start boxing up my own room.

And it's not like I even had any excuse to get out of it. Lori was away with her family. Their counselor had suggested going away together to reconnect as a family, so they were going to be gone the entire week. And since I didn't have a boyfriend, I felt completely alone. And depressed.

As soon as I got home on Friday, Dad was standing at the bottom of the stairs with an empty box, smiling. "Start with your closets. We have to declutter everything.

The realtor says it will show better." He looked at me for a moment. "You okay, Butterfly?"

I shrugged my shoulders.

"I know it's hard." He held out his arm, and I walked into it and let him hug me.

I took a deep breath and blew it out, taking the box from him. "I guess we have to do it, right?"

Dad leaned down and kissed me on the cheek.

"What was that for?" I asked.

Dad smiled. "I'm going to miss you."

"Oh, don't start that now. I'll end up crying the entire spring break."

Dad hugged me again. "Go on now. You're still going to have to help Anna."

I trudged up the stairs with my box, only to find three more sitting in my room. I sat down in the middle of the floor and just looked around. The boxes were ruining the view so I moved them out into the hallway, shut my door, and sat in the center of my room, taking in every detail. I flipped through the pictures in my mind of my mom in the room. I had lived in this room for most of my life. I didn't want to say good-bye again.

I was still just staring at my room when there was a knock at my door. I figured it was my dad checking to see if I was working, so I said, "Come in" as I crawled over to my bookcase and took a stack of books down.

"Beka?"

Dad stepped through the doorway. "How are you supposed to box things up if you have all the boxes piled out here?"

"Oh, yeah. I'll get it all done."

"Well, you have a visitor."

"Who?" I knew it wasn't Lori. Nancy maybe?

Josh stepped through the door. "Hey stranger."

My breath caught in my throat.

"Josh? What . . . I thought . . ."

Should I hug him or wave or what?

Dad looked between us and shook his head. "I'll be in the garage. Bye." He left and Josh took a step toward me.

"Surprised?" he asked.

I just nodded. Instead of feeling excited, I felt nervous and awkward and I couldn't believe he was really standing in my room. I wasn't sure what to do with myself, but then Josh took another step toward me and wrapped me in a hug. It was like every nerve in my body was alive.

"I don't understand. What are you doing here? I just saw Nancy yesterday."

Josh still had his arms around me, so I was looking up at him.

"I swore her to secrecy. When Mom and Dad changed their plans I decided to come home instead."

"I'm glad," I breathed.

"Me, too."

He was close enough. If I leaned forward just a little maybe he'd kiss me. Josh raised his eyebrows and cleared his throat. He stepped back and clapped his hands together. "So your dad says we're working today?"

"We?"

"I'm here to help. I'll do anything you need." Josh held his arms open wide and I smiled. "Now that's what I needed to see," he said.

I wrinkled my nose. "I haven't been doing a lot of that lately."

"How come?"

"I don't know. Everything?"

Josh held out his hand and I took it. "Good things are coming your way. I know it."

"Oh yeah? How do you know?"

He pulled me closer again and kissed my forehead. "I just do. Now I promised your dad I'd make sure you work. So where do we start?"

I laughed. "If you insist. That whole bookshelf has to be packed." I pointed with my other hand, not wanting to let go of the one that was holding his.

He walked over, pulling me with him, and looked it over. "You have a lot of butterfly things."

"I guess. Did you ever collect anything?"

"Yeah, rocks."

"Rocks?"

"Haven't you ever noticed how many different rocks there are? Wait." He dug in the pocket of his jeans and pulled out a smooth green stone. He dropped it into my hand. "See. Isn't that beautiful?"

I rolled the warm stone over in my hand. "It is."

"God had His people use stones to remind them what He had done for them. I guess that's what I've done. Stones remind me of things. Like that one. It means something special to me."

"What?"

"I'll tell you one day. But not today."

I held it out to him, and he took it and slipped it back in his pocket. "So why the butterflies?"

"I've just always liked them. And that's what my dad calls me." I pulled Josh over to the net cage where my new caterpillars were munching on leaves. "See. These little guys will be butterflies in a few weeks." Josh reached through the net and let one of the caterpillars crawl on his hand, and then pulled it back out.

"At school, I would have already dissected these things."

"Josh!" I hit him on the shoulder.

He laughed and slid the caterpillar back into its home. "What? I dissect everything."

"Gross. I love these little guys. I haven't raised them in a while, but I figured since this would be my last spring at home, I'd do it one more time."

"What do you do when they hatch, when they become butterflies?"

"Let them go."

Josh was looking at the caterpillars, and I was close enough to see his long, dark eyelashes above his eyes. Why couldn't I have lashes like that? He turned and caught me looking at him and smiled. I swear my heart skipped a beat.

"We better get busy."

"Yeah, I guess."

He looked at me for a long moment and then squeezed my hand and let it go. He went back into the hallway and dragged one of the boxes back inside. "So everything goes?"

"Everything on that shelf. I guess I'll start on a closet."

I spent longer than I meant to picking out some music to put on. It was a nice day, so I opened up the windows. I kept looking over to where Josh was packing books to remind myself that he was really there. My heart felt full just having him nearby. Because he lived so far away, I didn't let myself fantasize too much about him. But I was so good at keeping him at a distance that I was shocked by how quickly my heart closed that gap now that he was here.

We worked all afternoon, and just when I was thinking about closing the windows, Paul exploded into the room.

"I'm home."

"Paul!" I jumped into his arms, and he swung me around. Josh stood up and brushed his hands on his jeans, and as soon as Paul put me down Josh held out his hand.

"Hey. How are you, man?" They shook hands.

"Good." Paul looked between Josh and me and smiled.

"So how are you?" I asked.

"Good. Really good. School is hard, but I really like most of my professors. I think my chem professor is a hundred years old, but he's brilliant."

"My chem professor is a woman. My roommate has a big crush on her," Josh said.

Paul laughed and I frowned. "How cute is she?" I asked.

Josh laughed. "She's not my type." Paul and Josh exchanged a look, and I suddenly felt like I missed something.

"Dad needs some help in the garage, and he's ordering pizza," Paul said.

"Okay. I'm game." Josh clapped his hands together.

I followed Josh and Paul out, but then told them I was going to check on Anna and see if she needed any help. They went down the stairs talking and laughing.

"Hey Anna banana. Are you in here?" Anna's room looked like a tornado hit it, and only part of it had landed in boxes.

"I'm right here." Anna was sitting in a big pile of stuffed animals.

"Do you have those things in every corner of your room?"

"Pretty much."

"Are you going to keep them all?"

She shrugged and picked up a stuffed elephant with a purple scarf around its neck. She held it up. "Mom won this for me. At the fair. It was the summer before she died."

I went and kicked myself a spot on the floor and sat down next to her. It was strange to look at her, because even sitting in the stuffed animals she looked older. She wasn't such a little girl anymore.

"And this one." Anna pulled a red and purple hippo out of the pile. "Mom bought this one for me at the mall. She bought me a pretzel that day, too."

"Do you remember where you got all of these?"

"Most of them. Some of them are yours and Lucy's though."

"Do you want to keep them all?"

Anna nodded and tucked her red hair behind her ear.

"Then I guess we better box them all up. C'mon. One point for each one you can get in that box." I pointed to the box farthest away and Anna grinned.

"Two points," she said.

"Deal. Winner gets two minutes of free tickles."

Anna smiled and took aim at the box. In one flick of her wrist she sent the hippo in a smooth arc straight into the box. "Two for me."

"Hey, we're just getting started."

Anna ended up beating me, and after my two minutes of tickle torture were up we went downstairs in search of the pizza. Dad, Josh, and Paul were already eating. Anna went and climbed into Paul's lap, and I got a wink from Josh. Lucy took a bite of her pizza and actually talked for a while.

Once we finished Dad clapped his hands together. "Should we finish the garage?"

We all groaned, even Paul. "Let's go see a movie," he said.

"We've got all this work to finish. You need a break

already?" Dad shook his head like he couldn't believe what he was hearing.

"But you're going to make us work the entire spring break. We should at least get our nights off," Lucy said.

Dad looked around at each of us, everybody agreeing that Lucy had a point. Dad threw up his hands and dug his hand in his pocket. "Okay, I guess I better treat my labor well. Here, you all go. But don't stay out late; work starts first thing in the morning." Dad handed Paul some bills and he shoved them in his pocket.

"Daddy, you come with us. Please," Anna asked.

Dad lifted his eyebrows. "Nope. If you all are abandoning me, then I'm going to the video store and surprise Gabby."

Lucy and I went to change while Paul and Josh went to the computer to find out what was playing. We were out the door in less than fifteen minutes. We didn't want Dad deciding to send us into the attic or anything. I was thrilled when Josh climbed into my Dad's SUV with us. He slid in right next to me.

"I'm glad you're coming."

"Why not? I was just dying to see Skippy's Place."

"Sorry about that. Anna can only see PG," I said.

Josh leaned in and bumped my shoulder. "I'm just teasing. I don't care what we see."

Lucy leaned over the seat between Josh and me. "I'll take Anna to her movie. You all can see something else if you want."

I turned around. "Really? You wouldn't mind?"

"Nope. It's cool."

When we got to the theater, Anna and Lucy went to

see the kid movie while Paul, Josh, and I went to what they teased me was a "chick flick." I pointed out that no movie with a superhero could be a complete chick flick. I got sandwiched in between Paul and Josh, which only bothered me because I figured there was no chance of Josh taking my hand in front of my brother. But as soon as the lights went down I felt his arm move, and my hand was in his. I missed the first half of the movie daydreaming about what that could have meant, but in the end decided I'd just have to enjoy it and not think too much about it.

After the movie we went home, and since it was late, Josh said he needed to go. Everybody else said good-bye to him, but I hovered near the car.

"Can you take a walk?" he asked.

"Sure. It doesn't look like Dad's even home yet."

We walked out to the sidewalk and turned down the street. He didn't say anything right away, and I was overly concerned about what to do with my hands. I wanted to let them swing so that he could hold my hand, but it felt like it would be more natural to stick them in my pockets, especially since I was cold and hadn't worn my coat.

But before we had even reached the next house, Josh shrugged off his jacket and slipped it around my shoulders. I snuck a deep breath of the fabric, a mixture of cologne and popcorn from the movie.

"Thanks."

He let his arm linger around my shoulder but then let go. We walked for a while, not saying anything until we reached a small park.

"Remember those swings out at the retreat? Let's go swing."

We walked over and sat on side-by-side swings, each of us swinging as high as we could, then when we couldn't go any higher we dragged our feet on the ground and slowed down.

"I'm glad I came home," he said.

"Me, too. But I feel bad. Have you even seen your family yet?"

"I will." Josh jumped off the swing, crouched near the ground for a few minutes, and then came and sat back down.

"What was that?"

Josh held out his hand, and in it were two small white stones. "Take one. Now we'll both have a stone to remember tonight by."

I took it and turned it over in my hand. "I don't think I'll need any help remembering."

Josh turned and smiled at me, the dimple in his chin showing. "Me neither."

As warm and wonderful as I was feeling at that moment, a dark cloud snuck into my thoughts. How could this ever work? Now that he was here I didn't want him to leave.

I looked down and scuffed my shoe into the mulch under my feet.

"So, can I come help again tomorrow?" he asked.

I raised my eyebrow at him. "You sure you want to? My dad's liable to make you haul boxes."

"I don't mind. But I'd like you to spend the day with me on Monday."

"Monday? What's happening Monday?"

"A hike. And a picnic. With my family."

The air whooshed out of me like a deflated balloon. "What's wrong?"

"I just don't think . . . I mean they probably don't even . . ." I dropped my head back and looked up at the sky. I could barely make out the stars with the lights from the playground in the way.

"Talk to me. What's wrong?"

I told him about the spring break trip that I didn't go on because of everything with Mark and how I thought his parents probably didn't have a very good opinion of me. Josh shook his head the whole time I was talking.

"You owe them a chance to get to know you, don't you think?"

"I already know Nancy. I see her twice a week usually."

"They'll love you, Beka. How could they not?"

"Oh, I could think of a few reasons. They saw my picture in a paper. With another guy."

"But you're not with him anymore. That's what you told me."

"I'm not with him. It's beyond over."

"So?"

"So what if they hate me?"

Josh stood up and held his hands out to me. I took them and he pulled me up from the swing, lacing his fingers with mine. "It's important. I can't tell you all the details of why right now, but give them a chance. They'll love you."

He pleaded with his eyes and smiled at me until I

said, "Fine. I'll go." Then he broke into a wide grin. "But you'll have to talk to my dad tomorrow. I don't think he planned to let any of us have any days off."

"I'll talk to him."

Josh kept one of my hands, and we walked back toward my house. As much as I wanted a kiss, I knew he probably wouldn't, but I couldn't help hoping. When we got to my back porch he pulled me into a long hug, and I could feel his arm gently rubbing my back. Before I was ready he stepped back, and I slipped his coat off my shoulders.

"Thanks for your jacket." I held it out to him, and he took it and brought my hand to his lips and kissed it. He smiled and winked at me.

"See you tomorrow."

I was sure that my feet didn't touch the ground the whole way back to my room, but my dreams were another story. All night I dreamed that I was on one side of a cliff and Josh was on the other. I couldn't find a way to get across the cliff, and everything I tried completely failed. I woke up anxious until I realized that he was coming over and that for the time being, at least, we were on the same side of the cliff.

Not that I got to see him very much. We really worked all day. I still had more boxes to pack in my room, and I also had to help Anna, who wasn't getting much accomplished at all. Paul and Josh had been outside most of the day doing small projects for my dad.

Dad wanted to get as much done as he could before we listed the house. Inside we were only supposed to keep the bare necessities. By the time we all sat down to have the subs Gabby had ordered, I was wiped out and feeling sad. The walls were all going to be painted and the borders and wallpaper—all stuff my mom had picked out and put up—was all going to come down.

Paul and Josh came in and grabbed subs and sat down to eat with Anna, Lucy, and me.

"I talked to your dad and he said he'll set you free on Monday as long as I come and help paint this week."

I laughed. "See, you can get out of painting if I don't go."

"Not a chance. You're hiking."

*   *   *

It was Easter on Sunday, and after church we had a cookout at the house. I wished Josh had been there, but I knew he needed to spend the day with his own family. I didn't think much about what the hike would be like until I crawled into bed that night. Then I started worrying. I woke up late because of tossing and turning half the night, and was still rushing to get ready when Josh pulled into the driveway. I debated about what to wear, but I was really so nervous about spending the day with his family that I could barely make a decision. I finally just picked something and ran downstairs to pull on my hiking boots, which fortunately had not been packed.

I ran outside and reached the passenger side before I remembered my backpack, so I waved at Josh and ran back inside to get it. He laughed when I finally shut the car door.

"You sure you have everything?"

"I think so."

"It will be fine."

"Easy for you to say."

Josh drove to his house where his parents and Nancy were all waiting in the driveway. Not exactly the impression I wanted to make. We got out of Josh's car, and after quick hello's we climbed straight into their family Suburban. I had never felt so awkward in my life. I had this urge to explain the situation with Mark and prove to them that I wasn't some two-timing brat, but instead I just sat there like an idiot with a smile on my face.

Nancy laid her head back on the seat. "I just don't know why we have to leave so early."

"I think you'll manage," Mike said.

"So how's the packing going?" Nancy asked me.

I shrugged. "We have a lot more stuffed into that house than I thought. It's like every closet takes twice as long as you'd think. We still have to paint, too."

"But you're staying there until the wedding, right?"

"Yes, but Dad wants to put the house on the market by the end of the month. It's weird to think that someone else will be living there."

"I bet."

"What about you? Did you decide what you're going to do?"

Nancy smiled. "I'm going to South Africa for a year. Remember that Year of Your Life program I was telling you about? Well, I leave in June."

Nancy told me all about the program while Josh just listened. He was sitting close but his hands were folded in his lap. Not that I was expecting him to hold my hand in front of his family, but I still wanted him to. We arrived at a large campground, and Mike drove through it until he reached a parking lot at the end.

We all got out, and I pretended to be busy relacing my boots. We set out with Mike and Nancy in the lead, and then Josh, but Terri, his mom, hung back and started walking with me. I tried to smile, but all I could think about was our last conversation. I hoped she wouldn't bring it up.

"So, Beka. Tell me about yourself."

The trail was wide, and unfortunately that meant we could walk side by side. I wished Josh would slow down.

Where was I supposed to start?

"Josh and Nancy told us about your mom. I'm so sorry about that."

"Thanks." I never knew what to say when people said that. It was nice and all, but it was one of those things that made me feel even more awkward.

"What was she like?"

"She was a doctor." That's all I meant to say, but as soon as I did, it was like I couldn't stop talking. I told Terri all about her, everything she loved to do and how she was always interested in me even when I was being a brat. Terri was easy to talk to because she listened like she really cared. I don't know how long I talked, but when I ran out of things to say I felt weird all over again.

"It must have been hard to lose her. I hear your dad's getting married again."

I wondered how much else she knew about me.

"Yeah, her name's Gabby. She has a horse farm."

"I guess that's been hard, too."

"I don't know. I mean, it is, but it's different for me since I'll be leaving."

"But she'll still be your stepmother."

"I guess." Even though it was true, it wasn't how I preferred to think about it. I always saw her as my dad's fiancée rather than my new stepmother. It was easier that way.

We reached a steep spot and I moved ahead on the path now that it was too narrow to walk side by side. I was grateful for the quietness so I could gather my thoughts. I felt like I was on stage and I didn't know my lines. I didn't even want to consider what his mom probably thought of me. She seemed perfectly nice, so I couldn't decide why she made me so nervous. I figured it had to do with wanting her to like me, but being convinced that she wouldn't.

We hiked up along a path that had three separate waterfalls to the right of us. They were beautiful. We walked out on a rock ledge to see them better, and when we did, Josh appeared at my side.

"I think this is my favorite spot on this trail," he said.

I remembered hiking with Mark last year looking at waterfalls. The thought made me feel guilty.

"It's beautiful."

"We're going to stop up at the top and have lunch. You doing okay?"

"I don't know."

"They won't bite you."

"It's still weird."

"Thanks for doing it though."

Mike called for us to keep moving, and once we reached the top there was a small wooded clearing where Terri spread out a blanket for us to sit on. I wanted to take off my shoes, but I was afraid my feet might smell, so I just tried to rub my feet through the thick material of my socks. It didn't work very well.

They all talked during lunch, so I was able to just sit and listen, thank goodness. As I watched Terri and Mike talk and smile at each other, it made my heart ache for my mom. I knew my dad loved Gabby, but he had changed after my mom died, and he wasn't as easygoing. He was more serious. Mike seemed more like my dad used to be, cracking jokes and laughing. I didn't mean to feel sad about it, but I couldn't help myself.

If they noticed, no one said anything. Mike asked me about my dad's work, and they were all interested to hear about my dad's career change. We packed up the leftovers, and Mike stood up and clapped his hands. "Now for the fun part!"

Terri groaned and Nancy and Josh laughed. I looked around at them.

"What is he talking about?" I asked.

"You'll see." Josh winked at me, and we all followed Mike much farther up the trail. We walked along the stream and reached a spot where some other hikers were splashing in the water. They started above a ledge where two rocks formed a spot where the water rushed through. The hikers would slip between the two rocks and fall into a large pool below. It wasn't a huge fall, and after I watched four other people do it, it seemed pretty safe. But that didn't mean I wanted to do it.

Mike began unlacing his boots and pulled off his sweatshirt. He seemed more excited than anyone else. Terri, Nancy, and Josh all unlaced their boots while I stood there with my backpack watching them.

I walked over to the stream and bent down to put my hand in it. Just as I thought—the water was freezing.

"You coming?" Josh asked.

"You didn't warn me about this. I didn't bring extra clothes."

"You'll dry. We've got to hike back anyway."

Mike let out a war whoop, and we all turned to see him ride over the falls and splash into the water. He waded out wiping his face with his hands. "C'mon. I'm going again."

Nancy ran up, and this time Nancy emerged from the rocks and squealed all the way down. Josh looked at me.

"You're serious?"

He grinned.

"Fine, but if I drown it's your fault."

"You won't drown, I promise."

"What if I smash my head open?"

"Beka, there's plenty of room to land."

I unlaced my boots slowly and watched first Josh, then Terri also go over. I didn't want to admit that I was a little scared. But once I got my boots off I felt like I had to go. Josh grabbed my hand and pulled me up the trail and walked out into the stream with me. It was really cold at first, but not so bad after a couple of minutes. We let Nancy and a couple of others go in front of us, and Josh stood behind me with his hands on my shoulders. He pointed ahead of me.

"Just sit down and let the current take you right through there."

At that moment I was more bothered by sitting in the water than by taking the fall.

"Go ahead. I'll be right behind you," he said.

I dropped into the water, sucking in my breath, and I began drifting toward the two rocks standing guard at the point of no return. I held my breath and in a rush I was over, dropping through the air and landing with a splash. I popped above water and laughed.

"That was awesome!" I said. Mike and Terri were standing on the trail clapping and laughing.

Josh came over with a yell and was by my side a moment later. "Did you like it?"

I smiled and grinned. "I'm going again."

We probably spent at least an hour running up the small trail and taking the plunge. It was so much fun. Terri had packed an extra towel for me, so when we were all done she wrapped it around my shoulders. Something about all of us being soaked to the bone made me less nervous around them. The walk back was nice, and I was able to answer their questions and talk about my family and my faith without even having to think about it.

I was almost sorry to see it all end. After we all said our good-byes, Josh drove me back to my house and walked me up onto the front porch. We sat in the swing, right where he had handed me a box of stationery last summer and asked me to write to him. My heart felt fluttery even though I knew he wouldn't kiss me. I was still hoping he'd say something to reassure me that I really meant something to him.

"I should let you go change," he said.

I shrugged. "I'm used to it now."

Josh scooted closer and took my hand. "Thanks for doing this today."

"It was great. I had fun."

"Me, too."

"So when do you go back?"

"Not until the end of the week. I said I would come help paint."

"Well, I guess I'll see you again."

"Count on it."

He looked at me for a long moment and I held my breath, just watching his eyes.

"I better go," Josh said, breaking the moment.

Josh squeezed my hand and left, and I sat there, happy and frustrated all at the same time. Was it wrong to want more? And what was it exactly that I wanted anyway?

Spring break flew by, partially because Josh spent a lot of time over at the house, but also because we were so busy. By the end of the week we had stripped wallpaper, painted almost the entire house, and boxed everything that we didn't need to have in the house. Sometime during the week it stopped feeling like my home, and when we put all the furniture back in place, it looked more like a model home than like the place I had lived for the last ten years.

It made me sad. I was pretty sure that we were all feeling sad, because by Friday everybody was arguing with each other and even Dad seemed on edge. Since Josh was flying out the next day, Dad let me go out with

Josh Friday night to say good-bye. Before we left, Dad thanked him over and over for all of his help, but Josh kept shaking his head and saying he was glad to do it.

Josh took me out to dinner, a fancy Italian restaurant with candles and real tablecloths. In the middle of our dinner, the guy at the next table got down on his knee and proposed to his girlfriend. She cried and said yes, and the whole restaurant broke into applause. I just tried to smile and watch without looking as awkward as I felt. Thankfully, Josh changed the subject.

"I've had fun this week. I can't believe I have to go back tomorrow."

"I know. It stinks. And I'm so ready to be done with school."

"Did you decide what you're going to do?"

"Not for sure. I still have a little while before I have to have the contracts in."

"But you have some idea, don't you?"

I nodded. "I think I'm going to sign them. I think I'd regret not at least trying. Don't you think?"

"Probably. Is it what you want?"

I took a sip of water from my glass. "I love to sing. I love music. It's the only thing that I've done that seems to really fit. I feel like such a beginner, though. I think that's what's making me the most nervous. That they're making a huge mistake and they'll regret offering me the contract when they see what an amateur I am."

"I don't think they will. I bet that's why they're willing to give you a shot. Because you're not going to barge in there acting like you know everything."

"Definitely won't be doing that. It would be so hard

to leave my family, though. I worry about Lucy and Anna and what will happen to them."

"I'm sure they'll all miss you too."

"It's just kind of easy to sit here and talk about it, but I'd actually have to get on a plane and move to L.A. A huge city." I shook my head. "Can you see me living in L.A.?"

Josh smiled. "I think you'll do just fine. Will you still go to school?"

"Either UCLA or Asuza Pacific—it's a Christian university. But I'll only be able to go part-time."

"So will you still write to me when you're famous?"

"Famous. I'll never be famous."

"How do you know?"

"I guess I don't. I'm just going for the chance to sing. I don't think I could turn it down just to take the safe and easy road."

Josh raised his glass. "To new beginnings."

"To new beginnings." We clinked our glasses together.

At the end of the evening, Josh walked me to the door, and my heart ached just knowing that it would be months before I saw him again. He'd be back in time for my graduation and Dad's wedding, but I didn't want to be apart from him at all. He held my hand and took a step backwards.

"I better go. I still need to pack."

"Be safe. And call me."

"I will." He squeezed my hand and walked down the stairs. Then he stopped and turned around. He walked back up the stairs and in a second he wrapped his arms around me and kissed me.

He pulled back and rubbed his hand on my cheek. "I'm sorry."

"Don't be."

"I promised myself I wouldn't do that. I just . . ."

He looked in my eyes for a moment and then kissed me again. "Bye, Beka."

"Bye."

And then he was gone. His car pulled out of the driveway and disappeared, and I reached up and touched my lips, a smile spreading across my face.

I had gotten my kiss.

*   *   *

I floated inside and started up the stairs, but stopped when I heard my dad.

"Beka? Is that you?"

I followed his voice into the kitchen where he was sitting at the counter drinking a cup of tea, my contracts spread out in front of him.

"So how was your night?"

I wondered if he could tell that I had just gotten kissed. My cheeks felt warm, so that meant they were probably a little red.

"Good but totally depressing." I dropped my bag on the counter and climbed up on the stool next to him. "He leaves tomorrow morning."

"You mentioned that. He seems like a good guy."

"Yeah, a good guy who's three thousand miles away."

"Maybe." Dad held up part of the contract. "We should make a decision about this, you know."

"I know. Are you really okay with me moving out there?"

"I can't say I'm not concerned, but you'll be with Tony and Carlita."

"I don't know them very well."

"Are you saying you don't want to go?"

"No. It's just going to be such a huge change."

Dad leaned his elbows on the counter and looked at me. "Yes, it will. But change can be good. You'll be with family. And as long as you stay in school, I'll support you all the way. You know that."

"I know. I told Josh tonight that I think I'd regret not at least trying."

"Makes sense."

"And I can always come home if it doesn't work out, right?"

Dad winked at me. "Well, you can go to college. I'm not sure I want you just hanging around Bragg County doing nothing."

I laughed. "I think I'm going to do it. Really. I should do it."

Dad reached into his pocket and pulled out a pen. He clicked the top and handed it to me.

"What? Right now? You want me to sign it now?" I asked.

Dad smiled. "I know you, Beka. You've already made the decision. Go ahead so we can start getting all the details arranged."

I took the pen from him, and he slid the paperwork in front of me. I held the pen over the empty line with my name typed under it. I closed my eyes and signed. I opened them back up, but everything was the same. No fireworks, no theme music. Just Dad and me in the kitchen.

"What were you expecting?" Dad asked. He looked through the papers and found another spot for me to sign, and then he signed everything he was supposed to. "I'll mail these tomorrow." He stood up and hugged me for a long while.

"You'll come see me, right? And I can fly home?"

"Of course, Butterfly. Anytime you want to."

* * *

Going back to school on Monday was not fun. Nobody really wanted to be there, and it just felt like graduation was going to take forever to get there. Lori and I didn't get a chance to catch up until lunchtime.

I filled her in on my whole spring break and the two kisses I had been dreaming about.

"I'm happy for you, but it's kind of sad too. He's so far away."

"I know. Of course, now that I'm going to L.A., he won't be *as* far away."

"So what about you. How did things go with your family?"

Lori sighed. "Good, I think. They're talking, and he's not as angry anymore. It feels like things are getting better."

"I'm so glad. Has he moved back in?"

"Not yet, but that's what they're working toward. I'm just glad they're talking again. I was so afraid that they were really going to split up."

I caught a glimpse of Mark over Lori's shoulder, and without even looking she knew what I was looking at.

"Did you hear that Angela dumped him?"

I shook my head. "No. When?"

She shrugged. "Over spring break I think."

"He's coming over."

I watched Mark come toward us, his eyes on me. He slid in next to me.

"Hey, Beautiful." He had that smile on his face, but it didn't even faze me after looking at Josh's for a week.

"Mark. So how was your spring break?"

"Nothing special. What about yours?" He was leaning close, but instead of just trying to move away, I stood up.

"It was fine. We're going. Later."

We walked away, and I turned around to see Mark just sitting at the table staring at us. "Was that mean?" I asked Lori.

"No. You two have barely even talked lately."

"Well, at least I don't feel confused and torn anymore. Mark is very cute, but it's over. It's been over."

Lori left for class and Mark caught up with me on the way to theory.

"So how's your new song going?" he asked.

I frowned.

He looked at me. "The one for theory? I saw the class project list."

"It's going pretty good. Mark, what is this? You break up with your girlfriend, and I'm suddenly worth talking to again?"

"No. It's not like that."

"That's exactly how it is."

"Beka." Mark grabbed my elbow and pulled me to the side of the hall.

"I have nothing to talk to you about," I said.

"Give me a chance."

"You had your chance, Mark. More than one, actually." I pulled away and went into class, realizing we had a small audience. I ignored everyone and found a spot to sit and pulled out my notes. We had a free period to work, but instead of working on my song, I wrote lyrics to a new one. I figured if I was going to have to sing an entire album, I better learn to write stuff when I thought of it.

Too Late
This time around
I said good-bye
No regrets
And no more tears
Did you really think
I'd give it another try

It's too late
I'm moving on
It's too late
I'm finding out
Who I am without you

This time around
You won't change my mind
I've said good-bye
With no more tears

Journalism class was a madhouse, because not only did we have our regular editions to print, but we were also working on the special senior edition. I was surprised to admit it, but Mai had actually turned out to be a big help. It didn't matter to me that she was coeditor, and me giving her the job seemed to have changed something in her. She still wasn't nice, but she was no longer cruel.

She came over with a layout and spread it out in front of me.

"Do you think this piece should go here, or here?" She showed me the two options, and I held it in both spots to see what it would look like.

"Maybe here. If we did it here there'd be too much text on that page. Don't you think?"

"That's exactly what I said. Stupid sophomore."

"Who?"

"Stanley. He was arguing with me about it." Mai looked at me and then shrugged. "Whatever." She started to walk away, and I called her name before I had even thought through what I was going to say.

"Mai?"

She turned around.

"Can I ask you something?"

She frowned but walked back toward me. I pushed the chair out from underneath the other side of the table with my foot and she looked at it, but sat down.

"I was just wondering. You came to my youth group meeting a while back."

"So."

"So why? Why did you come?"

"We were invited."

"I know, but why did you come?"

Mai tucked her hair behind her ear and lifted her chin. "What, is it a crime?"

"No. It's just weird that you came that one night and never came back."

She watched me for a minute as if she was sizing me up. I shifted in my chair and waited.

"I just wanted the editor's job."

"Oh."

Mai stood up. "I need to finish this."

"Okay." She went back to the computers, where I could see her arguing with Stan again. At least now I knew.

*   *   *

The days passed by so slowly. Josh wrote to me regularly and called a couple of times, but he never mentioned our kiss. I wanted him to. I wanted some sort of official acknowledgment, especially since Mark was working overtime at school to flirt with me. It was flattering and made me feel good, but I wasn't about to give him another chance.

It was hard watching all the signs go up about prom. I didn't want to go, but in some ways I still felt like I was missing out on something important. I half expected Mark to ask but he didn't, and that made me feel bad all over again. The only good part was that our church had decided to throw a graduation formal on the weekend of graduation. It wouldn't be as big or fancy as prom, but I knew that Josh would be home to take me. If he wanted to. I couldn't bring myself to ask him, since the very first time we went out he told me he didn't like the girl to take the initiative. Even though Lori didn't go to our church, I convinced her to come with Brian.

Now I just had to hope that Josh would hear about it in time.

Josh came home for the summer just a few weeks before graduation. He took me out the first Saturday he was home, and it turned out I never needed to worry about the formal at all. Josh even brought it up.

"So I heard about this graduation formal they're having at Harvest."

I nodded, trying not to grin or look too eager.

Josh smiled. "Would you let me take you?"

The grin escaped and spread over my face. "I'd like that."

"Do you think I need a tux?"

I shook my head. "I don't think so, probably just a suit."

He nodded, put his fork down, and shifted in his seat. I did the same.

I thought maybe he didn't really want to go. "It's okay, you know. We don't have to go to it. It's probably going to be kind of lame anyway and . . ."

Josh shook his head. "What are you talking about? I want to go with you."

"Are you sure? You seem . . . upset."

Josh cleared his throat. "Well, it's not the formal. I've been trying to decide when the best time would be to talk to you."

My stomach tightened up, and I squeezed the napkin in my lap. Why would he ask me to go to the formal if he were going to break up with me? Not that we were anything official anyway.

He continued. "I was going to talk to you at graduation, sort of a graduation present or something but . . . there's going to be a lot going on, and maybe I should just do it now."

"Josh! Tell me already. I'll throw up if you don't."

Josh slipped an envelope out of his pocket and handed it to me. It was sealed and had my name across the front.

I just looked at it.

"Go ahead. Open it."

I slipped my finger under the flap and tore the top of the envelope open. I pulled out one single piece of paper.

"What is this?" I asked.

"It's a list of courses they've accepted for transfer."

I looked at him, confused.

"I'm transferring from Seattle Pacific."

I looked at the top of the paper and realized that it was letterhead from Asuza Pacific University. "This is in L.A."

Josh nodded.

"You're going to go to school in L.A.?"

Josh nodded again, watching me.

"Really?" I squealed. "But, but you love Seattle. Why would you . . ."

"You have to be in L.A., and it doesn't really matter where I take bio chemistry and all my other premed classes." He paused. "You're not happy."

"No, I am." I folded up the paper and put it back in the envelope. "It's just a lot of pressure."

Josh reached across the table and took my hand. "I don't want you to feel pressured. I just want us to have a fighting chance, and I don't think it's fair to you to have a boyfriend you only get to see a couple of times a year."

The word *boyfriend* seemed to echo in my ear.

He continued. "With my classes you still may not see very much of me, but it will be better than me staying in Seattle."

"Your parents? Are they okay with this?"

He nodded. "As I said, it doesn't really matter all that much where I take my classes. And that's why I wanted you to come hiking with us. So they could get to know you a little bit before I told them what I wanted to do." He squeezed my hand. "I thought you'd be happy."

"I am. I'm just so shocked. What if things go wrong though, and you did all this? I'd feel so horrible."

"Beka. Sweet Beka. We'll never go wrong if we follow God's lead. Where I go to college isn't changing the direction God's taking me. I'd just like the chance to walk toward Him while being close to you. I don't want to be away from you."

"Me neither." I smiled. "So, this means what? Are we . . ."

Josh grinned. "Beka. Will you be my girlfriend?"

I laughed. "I thought you'd never ask." I couldn't remember ever feeling happier.

*   *   *

The last week of school before graduation was a lot of half days and some exams. I had been so busy that I kept putting off dress shopping. I needed one for the formal and one to wear under my cap and gown. Gabby promised to take me out to find dresses, and so I was waiting in the kitchen for her on Wednesday, hoping that I'd still be able to find something halfway decent. She was late, and I was pacing around when I finally saw her pull up in her truck. She got out and then pulled a big box out of the seat.

A moment later she came into the kitchen.

"I'm sorry. I know I'm late." She put the box on the counter. I figured it was something for the wedding. Our dining room was already overflowing with gifts for the two of them.

I grabbed my bag. "I thought we'd go up to Taylor's Crossing. Their stuff is nicer."

"Okay. But open the box first."

I looked at her and then the box. "It's for me?"

Gabby jutted her chin toward it. I pulled the top off and moved the tissue paper aside. Inside was the purple silk dress. I sucked in my breath. "It's the dress from the shop. From Caroline's."

Gabby smiled and sighed loudly. "I was so worried it wouldn't get here in time. Caroline had your measurements, so she altered it for you. I think the only problem was the length. It should fit perfectly, but you'd still better check it."

I picked it up gently and slid it out of the box, holding it out in front of me. "I love this dress." I looked up at her. "Thank you."

Gabby smiled and dropped her head. I laid the dress over the box and went over and wrapped my arms around her. She seemed surprised at first but then she hugged me back. "You didn't have to do that. But I'm glad you did," I said.

"It's just my way of, well, thanking you for giving me a chance."

I stepped back and looked at her, tears in her eyes. I should have given her more of a chance than I did. "Thank you." I pulled the hanger out of the bottom of the box and slipped the dress on the hanger. "I still need a dress for graduation though."

Gabby jumped just a little. "Let's go then. Are we taking Lucy and Anna?"

"Nope. It's just you and me."

Gabby grinned, and I followed her out the door. I actually had fun with Gabby, and I felt better knowing how good it would be for Lucy and Anna to have her around. At least they wouldn't be on their own with Dad, and she really did seem to care about them. And me. I managed to find a pale blue sundress that would work under my cap and gown, and on the way home, I got a chance to talk to Gabby about Lucy. I didn't share any details, but just told her that Lucy had been having some trouble at school and she should keep her eye on her.

*　　　*　　　*

I woke up the day of my graduation to hear rain pounding on the roof. The sun was nowhere to be seen, and it was gray and dreary. I was disappointed because Friday had been sunny and beautiful, but at the same time, it almost seemed fitting. I kind of felt gray and dreary myself. My room had been all but emptied of all my belongings, which were either being shipped out to California or moved out to Gabby's house. Everything had changed, and I didn't have any choice but to keep moving forward.

I got ready slowly and tied a blue ribbon around my head as a headband. I slipped my white gown over my head and looked at myself in my dresser mirror. I still looked the same. My hair was shorter and more stylish, but I still had the same freckles, the same nose, and the same eyes. I wondered what my mom would have said to me. It was my first big event, a major rite of passage that she wouldn't be here for. She would have been happy, and probably would have cried a fair amount. It struck me that if she had still been around, L.A. wouldn't be happening, because Gabby wouldn't have become part of our lives, and without Gabby there would no Tony. It seemed wrong for good things to come from the worst thing that had ever happened to me.

When it was time to go we all ran out to the car to keep from getting soaked. Once we reached the high school, we found that the ceremonies had been moved into the gymnasium. Paul gave me a hug when I was leaving to go line up and whispered, "I'm so proud of you" in my ear. It made me smile. I ran off to find Lori, who was already in line.

I gave her a hug. "I don't know what I would have done if you hadn't come to this school when you did."

"I don't know what I would have done if I hadn't found you crying in the bathroom."

I laughed. "We'll still be friends, right?"

"Always. We can write and e-mail."

"It won't be the same."

"I know. But we're sisters because of Jesus. You won't ever be able to get rid of me." Lori grinned.

"Aww. Man," I teased.

"Five minutes, people. Five minutes," Mrs. Brynwit yelled as she walked down the rows of students. She stopped next to Lori and me. "Miss Madison."

"Mrs. Brynwit."

"Well, I hear congratulations are in order for you."

"Yes, ma'am."

"Make Bragg County High proud."

"Yes, ma'am."

She nodded at me then stuck out her hand. I shook it and she bellowed, "Three minutes. Let's move it," and moved down the hallway.

I looked at Lori. "I bet that was hard for her to do."

"Oh, definitely." Lori nodded.

I gave Lori another quick hug and then went off to find my place in line. The music played, and we all filed into our seats and listened as they awarded some honors and introduced the valedictorian, Tracey Showalter. I was pretty sure that she had never even left school property during high school. She gave a nice speech, and then they began calling names. I watched Mark walk across the stage and get his diploma. It was strange because now it was totally different when I looked at him. I walked up with my row and was totally focused on not tripping as I walked up the stairs and took my diploma. I turned like they had told us to so we could get our picture taken, and when I did, I saw my family waving at me and lifting their arms in silent cheers. I walked offstage and watched Lori go just a few minutes later.

And then it was over. My dad and the rest of my family came over to me.

"Let me see this thing," Dad said, taking my diploma. "Beka. Have you looked at this?"

"No." I took it from him and saw that it read "Amy Renee Marks." "I guess I better go find her." I smiled.

It took a little while to sort out the diplomas because Amy didn't have mine, she had someone else's. While I was waiting I felt a pair of hands go over my eyes.

"Josh?"

"No, it's Mark."

I turned around to see Mark looking disappointed.

"I just wanted to say congratulations. In case I don't see you again."

"Thanks. You too."

Josh came up next to me and slipped his arm around my waist. It was cute that he was being protective.

"Well, bye, Beka."

"Bye." I waved at Mark and then turned to Josh. "Hey, you."

Josh leaned down and touched my nose with his. "I have to go, but I'll see you tonight, okay?"

I smiled and nodded and went off to find my family again. When we got outside it had stopped raining, so I asked my dad to go by the cemetery for me. Paul had left his cap on Mom's gravestone when he graduated, and I wanted to do the same. They all waited in the car as I picked my way out to the grave site, trying not to sink into any mud. Being careful didn't help though, because my heels got covered in mud anyway.

I slipped my cap off my head and took my tassel off. I put the cap on top of the gravestone and straightened the pot of flowers that had blown over.

I glanced around and saw that no one was around. "Mom. I wish you were here. And I miss you so much. But things are okay. Good, even. I graduated today. I wish you could have been there. I won't ever forget you. No matter what. I love you, Mom."

I swallowed the lump in my throat. I didn't want to leave, but didn't know what else to say either. I walked back to the car and took off my muddy shoes before getting inside. Paul found a plastic bag to put them in, and we went home to have lunch. And I had a dance to get ready for.

I came down the stairs and found my dad and Paul in the living room playing a game of chess.

"So what do you think?" I asked.

They both looked up, and the looks on their faces made me blush.

"Wow. So that's what Gabby's been talking about," Dad said.

I twirled around.

"I'm glad it's Josh you're going with," Paul said. "Otherwise I think I'd have to go with you."

Dad stood up. "So I get to take pictures this time?" He shook his head and walked toward me, pulling me into a hug. "I can hardly believe that you're the same little girl." His voice cracked. "Your mom would have loved this."

I felt the tears sting my nose, and I tried not to let them fall down my cheeks. Because then I'd have to go redo my makeup, and I was ready to go. I heard the doorbell ring and Dad pulled away and smiled at me, putting his hand under my chin. "I hope you have a wonderful time." His eyes were rimmed with tears, and I felt this overwhelming urge to cancel going to L.A. and stay home. But it wasn't really that I wanted to stay home, I just didn't want things to change between us, to put a whole country between my dad and me. Not that we hadn't had problems, but I finally felt good about our relationship, and now I would be leaving.

"I'll get the door," Paul said, and when my dad and I came into the foyer, Paul and Josh were talking. They stopped when they saw me.

Josh just stared for a long minute, and then his face softened into a smile. He held out his hands, and I took them while he leaned in and kissed me on the cheek. "You have never looked more beautiful," he whispered in my ear.

I let go of one hand, and we let my dad snap a whole roll of film. Josh was a good sport about it all.

"Beka tells me that you transferred. That you'll be going to school in L.A.?" Dad asked once he had slung the camera over his shoulder.

Josh cleared his throat. "Yes, sir."

"And you and Beka?"

I felt fire lick my cheeks, and I dropped my head, wishing I could crawl under the carpet and hide.

"Well, sir. I'll still be in medical school, so I won't have a lot of time. But this way, we can see where God takes us and be close enough to each other to be . . . committed to one another," Josh said. I could tell he was nervous, because he was squeezing my hand tightly and he kept pressing his lips together.

"So you plan to date?"

"With your permission sir, yes, I'd like to see her as much as we can. Of course, we'll both have pretty busy schedules."

"So how serious is this?" Dad asked.

I couldn't stand it anymore. "Da-ad. Please." Paul stifled a laugh, but winked at me.

Josh looked around for a second then said, "I'm very serious, sir, both about your daughter and following the Lord in His plan."

Dad looked at him and then nodded and held out his hand. Josh shook it, and then Dad hugged me. "Have fun tonight."

"Thanks."

When we finally escaped onto the porch I burst out laughing. I leaned over at the waist and held my hands over my stomach. I couldn't even laugh delicately; they were loud and hiccupy laughs. Josh watched me like I was nuts and then began laughing too.

"Are you okay?" he asked when I had gained my composure.

I nodded, dabbing at my eyes so that I didn't smear my makeup. "I had no idea he was going to do that, I swear."

Josh shook his head. "It's okay. But I'm really glad it's over with."

I nodded and smiled. "Me, too."

Josh held out his elbow and I took it. "We should get out of here before your dad thinks of any more questions."

*　　　*　　　*

We met Lori and Brian for dinner and had a lot of fun. Brian and Josh got along well, so it gave Lori and me time to talk. We drove to the church and I was thrilled with what we found there. Someone had gone all out to make everything look beautiful. There were flowers and shimmery white balloons everywhere. One part of the foyer was set up to take pictures, and when we walked into the sanctuary, the chairs normally set up for the service had been cleared away and in their place were tables set up with candles and more balloons and flowers. They were arranged in a full arc around the stage where a full band was already playing.

Instead of just playing music and dancing though, they had brought in a couple that taught us all to swing dance. We spent the first hour of the dance getting lessons and practicing with different partners. I had never danced like that before, but had always thought that it looked like fun. Every once in a while I looked around for Josh. It was so cute to see him counting steps and concentrating so hard. We learned a two-step and a three-step dance, and when the lesson was over the band came onstage and played.

Finally we got to choose our own partners, and I stood near the side of the dance area, looking around for Josh. I couldn't find him anywhere, and just when I was about to give up and go find something to drink, I felt a pair of arms go around my waist. I turned around and looked up at him.

"I thought I had lost you," I said.

He shook his head. "Nah. I don't see that happening."

"Should we try this?" I asked.

Josh rubbed his hands together and then held them out. "I'm ready." We counted out the steps until we seemed to get the hang of it. The instructors kept circling the floor, helping us correct anything we were doing wrong. We couldn't do any of the fancy stuff they had showed us in the beginning, but it was a lot of fun. Lori and Brian were laughing and smiling, too.

We really spent most of the night dancing, and by the end I was so tired that I dropped into one of the chairs at the table. Lori came and sat down beside me.

"This was so great. I'm glad you wanted me to come."

"Did Brian like it?"

She nodded. "Yeah. He's not the best dancer in the world, but I can totally live with that."

I laughed. "I still can't believe we graduated today. It's really done."

"I know. So you're not working this summer?"

I shook my head. "I'm taking some guitar and some music composition lessons to get ready for L.A."

Lori gave a sad smile. "We won't see each other very much."

"I know. But we'll try. As much as we can."

The lights were turned on in the sanctuary, and they began clearing the tables and putting all of the balloons in the foyer. Josh and Brian came over.

"We better go. They're trying to clean up," Josh said.

I groaned. "I don't even want to move."

"I'll help you." Josh held out his hand. I took it, and he pulled me to my feet and caught me in his other arm. We walked out into the foyer where Josh pulled two balloon strings and handed one to me. Then we went outside.

"I had a great time, Beka."

"Me, too."

"One, two, three," he said, and we let go of both the white balloons and watched them drift into the night. Josh put his arm around me and we watched until we couldn't see them anymore.

It was sort of how I felt. Like I was about to drift off not knowing exactly where I was going to end up.

"You know, L.A. doesn't seem as scary to me now that you're going, too," I said.

"Good. You shouldn't be scared. You're in God's hands, and there is no better, or safer, place to be," Josh said.

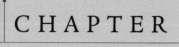ony and Carlita came into town a few days before the wedding. There seemed to be lists of stuff that still had to be done, but by the morning of the ceremony, everything was ready. It had been fun having Carlita around, because she seemed so excited that I was coming that it made me feel better about moving in with them.

Dad had chosen Paul as his best man, and Tony and a couple of my dad's good friends from work were his groomsmen. Carlita was the matron of honor and Lucy and I were bridesmaids. Anna had insisted on being a junior bridesmaid because she said she was too old to be a flower girl. After we had all gotten our hair done, we went to the church to get ready for the ceremony. Megan was the photographer for the wedding, so she had been around all morning snapping pictures of us getting ready. She gave me a hug and told me she was praying for me. It was nice, because even though I hadn't told anybody how I was feeling, Megan seemed to sense that I was having a hard time.

Seeing Gabby in her wedding dress was strange, and I watched her from the doorway, trying to sort out all the emotions that came flooding through me. She was so happy, and I wanted to be happy for her. But I just mostly felt sad. I saw Lucy standing in the corner, also watching Gabby, with mixed emotions on her face. When I caught her eye, I gestured for her to follow me to another room. We found a room that wasn't being used and slipped inside. I sat down and she picked a seat near me.

"You doing okay?" I asked.

She shrugged and smoothed down her dress. "It's just so weird."

"I know."

"But it's different for you. You're going away," she said.

"I know."

"We're going to be living with her."

"Lucy. That's not exactly news."

"But today it seems so real."

I scooted my chair closer. "Lucy. How are you doing with, the other thing?"

"Ethan?"

I nodded.

"Better, I think. I'm really glad school's over. I hated seeing him. It was like being reminded of it every day."

"But Julie? Has that been helping?"

Lucy nodded. "Yes. We don't agree about it, but that's okay. I can talk to her about other stuff. About all this."

"What do you mean you don't agree?"

"She still thinks I should report what happened."

"And you?"

"We were a couple. I went up there. If I hadn't done that, then nothing would have happened."

"But you're going to keep seeing her, right?"

"Yeah. Dad said I could go as long as I wanted. I think Julie's going to make me tell Dad, though."

"She won't make you."

"You know what I mean."

I nodded. "I'm glad I'm not Ethan."

Lucy smiled. "Yeah. So you think I should tell Dad, too?"

I nodded. "Yeah. I mean, I'm glad you aren't going to those parties anymore, but I don't want to see you get tempted to get into all of that again. Dad knowing about it may help with that. Of course," I half grinned, "he may not ever let you go anywhere again."

She shrugged. "I didn't want to ruin his wedding, you know?"

"Yeah. There's no rush. At least you don't seem as upset anymore," I said.

"I'm not. I'm going to youth group again, of course. And things are better with God. I think." She shrugged again. "I'll be okay, if that's what you're asking."

"That is what I'm asking."

"It's getting better. And I have a clean bill of health—physically anyway. And Julie will help me with the other stuff."

The door came flying open, and Anna popped into the room. "You have to come for pictures." She bounced away.

I laughed and shook my head. "I think she's doing better than all of us."

Lucy rolled her eyes. "She won't shut up about living with the horses."

"They should just let her have one of the stalls instead of a room," I said.

"She'd probably like that." Lucy stood up then stopped when we got to the door. "Beka? Do I have to call her Mom?"

I stopped and turned toward her. "No. Not unless you want to. That's up to you."

Lucy took a deep breath and nodded. "Good. Because I don't think I'm ready for that."

"Me, neither. But someday you might be."

"You think?"

"You never know. God knew all of this was going to happen to our family. And He can take something bad and make something good out of it." I hugged her and held her as long as she'd let me. When she pulled back, she wiped a tear away.

"Can I still call you?" she asked.

"You better." I winked at her. "C'mon. Let's go smile for the camera."

"It's going to be a long day," she said.

*　　*　　*

And it was a really long day. Watching Gabby walk down the aisle and listening to them say their vows to each other was strange. I watched it as if I was watching a movie of someone else's life. It was happening, but it was like it was happening to someone else. I watched my dad, how happy he was, the smile on his face, and it helped me feel better about the whole thing. At the end of the ceremony, when the pastor prayed over them, I offered my own prayer for them.

Lord, Thank You for making my dad happy again. For giving him someone so that he doesn't have to be alone anymore. Give them joy together. And help the rest of us to find our way. Be with us all as we start this new part of our lives.

*　　*　　*

The reception was a lot of fun. Lori, Brian, Josh, and Nancy were all there, so it was fun hanging out with them. Especially since Nancy was leaving for South Africa in just a few days. Tony asked me for a dance and told me how glad he was that I was coming to L.A. and how different I was from so many other teens out there. I think he was trying to compliment me, but it made me feel a little nervous. How backwards would I look to everyone in Southern California?

Dad danced with me and told me how proud he was of me, and he thanked me for supporting him and being so wonderful. I felt a little bad because I remembered all the times that I tried to stop the whole thing from happening.

Paul cut in while I was dancing with Dad.

"You better stay in touch. Let us know how you're doing."

"I'm not leaving for a month."

"It will go by like that." He snapped his fingers. "Just stay close to God, and you'll be fine."

"I will. You know, the more I learn about God, the more I learn that I have a lot to learn."

Paul laughed. "That's just as it should be."

"If it weren't for God I wouldn't have ever signed that contract. It's like the scariest thing I've ever done, but I know that I'm not alone."

"You're not."

"Yeah, but now I really know it. Down here." I tapped the center of my chest. "It's like some big adventure. I don't know where it's all going to end up, but I know He does. Right?"

"Right. You've come a long way in just two years. You amaze me."

I smiled. "Ditto."

As soon as Paul and I parted, Josh slipped in front of me.

"My turn," he said.

I wouldn't dream of arguing with that.

*   *   *

Dad and Gabby left on their honeymoon, and Paul and I had to drive Anna and Lucy and all the presents out to the farm. I was driving Paul's car, and I was by myself.

I took one of the flower arrangements from one of the tables with me and drove by the cemetery.

I put the flowers in front of Mom's grave marker and smiled when I saw my limp mortarboard wilted over the top of the stone.

"I guess you know what today was. I thought you'd like the flowers. Dad and Anna are happy, and the rest of us, we'll be okay. So much is happening. Good things. But I still miss you. I always expected you to be there for graduation and when I left for college. And my own wedding one day. You'd like Josh. He's the kind of guy moms would like. I think Dad's nervous about us being in L.A. and him here, but you don't have to worry about Josh.

"I'm going to be a singer. Remember how you always told me I should sing, and I never would? You were right all along. I want to do it all the time now. I could be a big flop, but I don't really care. At least I don't right now. Because I actually get to try. I promise I'll come back to visit.

"I wish you could tell me what heaven's like. I can't even imagine what you might be doing. I hope you love it. I love you, Mom."

July 31

I'm on the plane. Dad cried at the security check-point, and Paul kept hugging me, like he didn't know what else to do. Even though I'm scared out of my mind, I feel like things couldn't be better. Gabby and Dad are now partners at the new Twin Oak Ranch, and Dad already has some big business plan for expanding the ranch. He says he doesn't miss the bank at all. Lucy and Anna seem good and will both go to new schools. Anna's a little bummed about not being with some of her friends, but she makes friends so easily that I doubt she'll have any problems. I'm really glad Lucy's moving schools, and I think she is too. Maybe it will also give her a fresh start.

Josh won't be coming out to L.A. for three more weeks, and even then I know he's going to be busy. But he'll be there! That's what matters. Dad and Tony have already talked about my "new rules," but they're not too bad. Considering if I had gone away to college I wouldn't have to ask to go out or have anybody checking to see what time I came home. But it's L.A.—a huge city—so I'm not complaining about them—yet.

Being eighteen doesn't feel any different, but being on this plane with no grown-ups makes me feel older. I can't even imagine what it's going to be like to make an album, to work with marketing and production people. But Tony works there, and since he's now my uncle, I know he'll watch out for me.

I always used to think that God had done some terrible thing by letting my mom die. I do wish it hadn't happened, but I look at everything that's happened because of it, and I can't help but think that God knew what He was doing all along, even though I didn't understand it. It's like everything that happened helped me to become me. And I've never needed Him so much. I'm glad Tony, Carlita, and Josh will be in L.A., but I only feel really safe because God will be there, too. Surely He has a plan for me in all of this. I can't wait to see what it is.

The Becoming Beka series

Beka has been trying to move on with her life since her mother's tragic accident, but it feels like she's going nowhere fast. Things are not so good at home. Beka's brother and sisters won't leave her alone. Her scary dreams keep coming back. And worst of all, Beka has a secret she can't share with anyone, especially not her family.

The Masquerade
ISBN: 0-8024-6451-3
ISBN-13: 978-0-8024-6451-4

When Beka heads back to school with a newfound faith, she expects some special feeling, some enlightenment, something different. But what she feels is . . . nothing. In fact, what she faces is a series of tough choices. For some reason Gretchen, the most powerful and popular girl in school, takes an interest in Beka, and Beka finds herself enjoying the popularity. But Gretchen's attention comes with a price.

The Alliance
ISBN: 0-8024-6452-1
ISBN-13: 978-0-8024-6452-1

Life can be confusing. Especially when it comes to boys. As Beka's junior year winds to a close, Josh and Mark are both vying for her affections. Since Josh is going to college in Seattle in the fall it seems clear that Mark, a fellow junior, is her best chance for finally having a boyfriend. But with her dad's strict rules about spending time with guys, Beka's left frustrated and wondering if she'll ever have a boyfriend.

The Passage
ISBN: 0-8024-6453-X
ISBN-13: 978-0-8024-6453-8

Finally—Beka's senior year! As usual, Beka's life is crowded with people and challenges. Gabby still has her heart set on Dad. For some reason, Mai is trying to make friends with Lucy. Mark's smiles make Beka melt, but she also likes Josh, who is away at college. And will Beka decide to go to college next year, or will she choose to pursue an exciting and surprising new opportunity?

The Reveal
ISBN: 0-8024-6454-8
ISBN-13: 978-0-8024-6454-5